CAPTIVE

BOOK 2 OF THE VUKASIN SAGA

B.D. Snowden

GEEKY GOTH PRESS

ISBN: 0692706259
ISBN-13: 978-0692706251

DEDICATION

This is dedicated to the readers. Without you, I am just a
crazy lady telling stories to myself.

ACKNOWLEDGMENTS

I couldn't have pursued my writing without the patience of my family. I'd also like to thank 8th Street Coffee House for allowing me to hole up in a corner and supplying me with caffeine .

CHAPTER ONE

Maria Russo wrapped the thin blanket around her shoulders in a desperate attempt to ward off the chill of the night. She tried to be thankful that her small cell was at least dry. *Madre dio.* There was little enough to be thankful for these past few months. Or maybe it was weeks…or even years. The passage of time had little meaning when you marked it based on the screams of your fellow captives and the brutality of your jailors.

Her old life seemed almost like a dream. She had just gotten off a double shift as a nurse at the trauma center in Pisa, Italy. Her bag was packed, and despite being exhausted, she hopped into her little car to make the drive to the coast. Gio, her fiancé, was supposed to meet her at *Nonno's* house for their engagement party. She had hoped to be able to relax by the ocean for a few days.

About thirty minutes into the countryside, Maria had pulled out her cell phone to call Gio to let him know she was on her way. He had just answered when she had to swerve to miss a huge man standing in the middle of the winding road. She was fairly certain she had screamed as she crashed into a ditch. Before Maria could clear her aching head, two sets of hands were pulling her from the wreckage. She could hear Gio screaming on the phone asking if she was alright.

At first she thought the men were trying to help her. She tried to tell them she was bruised but all right, but they injected her with something that quickly stole her consciousness. When she woke she was in a room with several other women from around the world and discovered she was no longer on her planet, Earth.

At first things hadn't been too bad. The women were mostly ignored. While the room Maria woke up in had effectively been a prison, they had had regular food and drink. There had been the privacy of a real bathroom and real beds with blankets and pillows.

The room itself had been beautiful. Murals covered many of the walls. Plush rugs covered the floors, and there had been comfortable furniture placed around the space.

More than anything, she missed not being

alone. It was a sad testament to Maria's life now that she thought longingly about a gilded cage. Life was all relative after all. If one had to be imprisoned it was better to be in a comfortable one where you weren't abused daily, even if you didn't have a change of clothes for days.

After the Vukasins, as Maria learned the name of the alien species that took her, brought in a woman and her small child, things had changed pretty rapidly. The women were no longer just quietly compliant. She, along with the rest of the women, refused food and became difficult. They had hoped it would get them out of the palace room so they could find a way back home. It had worked in a way. The women were sent to different households to live. Maria sincerely hoped the other women fared better than she had.

Unfortunately, crashes and kidnapping seemed to follow Maria. Her caravan had been attacked right after they had dropped off the woman known as Sara. The men guarding her fought valiantly. The last soldier had tried to make a break for it, urging the beasts that pulled their carriage to speed away. They shot him from afar. It was his death that caused her transportation to crash.

As she tried to crawl out of the wreckage, numerous men wearing a snake-looking symbol surrounded her. The look in their eyes had her attempting to cover herself, even though her hospital scrubs were very modest. They looked at her as if she was naked and they were waiting their turn to have a go at her. That look made her freeze in fear. A part of her still wonders if she might have escaped if she had reacted sooner. Ah well, that was a moot point anyway. *Nonno* always said, "The past can't be rewritten, so apply your pen to the present."

*****

Heavy footsteps echoed in the stone hall outside of her cell, bringing Maria back to the present. Maria tensed, ready to fight. She had already been experimented on and raped. She was no longer what anyone would consider "pure." The irony was not lost on her that had she and Gio not waited in deference to both of their conservative Catholic families that the Vukasin warriors sent to retrieve women would probably have chosen someone else since they had been instructed not to take mated females. Not that Maria would wish this fate on anyone else, but it was sometimes difficult not to wallow in the what if's of life.

The footsteps stopped outside of Maria's door. She could hear the beep on the crystal lock signaling the guard's DNA was accepted. She still wasn't quite sure how the device scanned the DNA. If she could figure that out, she might be able to figure out a way to bypass it. Even if she figured that out, she was a long way from escaping.

Maria hated this daily ritual. She hated her cell, but at least when she was alone here she felt relatively safe. Maria stood. She had a better chance of inflicting damage when she was standing—not that she was ever able to inflict much. The guards were large even by the huge Vukasin standards. But Maria refused to let them take her without a fight. She was fairly certain that the day she quit fighting was the day she would die.

"Come and get me, *bastardo*."

CHAPTER TWO

"Ghaleb, we know for sure that Maria Russo and the first human are missing, most likely at the hands of the Tanis traitors." Megan stared down the *Khalon* of the Vukasin Empire. "Himeko has reported that there are at least three native women that have gone missing in the last few weeks, and I am hearing rumors of more in other districts."

"Megan, I am doing what I can to locate those women, but honestly they are not the priority right now. I have—"

"Not a priority!" Megan banged her fist on the council table, causing every representative to flinch. Her ghost lions growled and paced in the corner. Thankfully, one of the three had begun spending the majority of its time with Megan's daughter Abby. They all had come to recognize when her temper was about to be unleashed, and she was very protective of the women...all women, human and Vukasin alike. Hopefully none of the clan representatives would have bite marks after this session, unlike the first session after the *Mate Avi Keiger.*

To his credit, Ghaleb didn't let the little virago intimidate him. Vukasin men dwarfed her barely over five foot frame, but she still managed to scare the giant men most of the time. He gave her a steady stare. "Our government is still in chaos. We are still trying to figure out just how deep Bel's treachery goes. We are on the brink of civil war. As much as I would like to, I cannot put the concerns of an entire planet after the needs of a few individuals."

Megan crossed her arms, "I concede that your position does not allow you to devote the necessary time and resources to this search, but I maintain that the fate of these women needs to be a priority. As such, the Tiaret clan will devote our resources—"

"No. I cannot allow that."

"Allow?!" Kia and K'ah's hackles went up. K'ah stretched high on the wall, his claws gouging deep lines as he stared intently at the council table. The silent councilors weren't sure if the growl came from Megan or the cats. "You forget, *Khalon*, that I carry the Spear."

"You want to rule? Be my guest!" Ghaleb's voice echoed through the chamber.

"I don't want to rule, but if you don't get your head out of your—" Megan shouted.

Cutting Megan's diatribe off, Ghaleb growled. "Reijo, do something about your mate!"

Reijo just smiled and held his hands up to his sovereign, but he did lay a gentle hand on Megan's heaving shoulder.

"*Jinaria*, it would be foolish of the government to release the Tairet from their service as the Empire's warriors. Experienced soldiers win wars." Reijo's hand trailed down to Megan's hand, bringing her fingers to his lips. His gentle coaxing helped to remove the tension in her body.

Megan sighed, and despite the frown that remained on her face, Reijo knew that his argument had reached her.

"I can't just leave them, Ghaleb. I have to do something. You have to do something." Megan's eyes swept the council chamber. "It was the decisions and actions of this council that caused the issues our women are facing today. It is the duty of the *Khalon* and this council to fix it, and that starts with the missing women."

Ghaleb pushed away from the council table. Running his hand through his messy hair, he paced. "I can't give you an entire clan. By the moons, I'm not even sure I could spare a single unit. Revolts have broken out along the desert border with many of the Tanis clan. Our intelligence says that more than just the Tanis clan was involved with the plot against the throne." Ghaleb's eyes went to his old friend Reijo. The frustration and uncertainty flashed just briefly before his blank mask was in place once again as he turned to face the council. "Does anyone have any suggestions?"

The council eyed each other, not knowing what to do. Ghaleb was a ruler they understood, but by ancient law, Megan could usurp power at any time because the gods gifted her with the Spear of Authority. Like many politicians, the council members were more concerned with maintaining their position and power than advocating for the people. They were in unfamiliar territory with two potential ruling bodies and no direction of who out ranked whom.

Ghaleb nearly called an end to the meeting because no progress was being made. He wondered if he should try to find a way to dissolve the council, even though it had been his grandfather who had created it as a protection for the people, should Ivailo fall.

Just as he was about to dismiss everyone, Elod spoke up.

Elod had recently been appointed as representative to the council for the Tiaret clan. Reijo had felt that because he was Megan's mate he needed a less biased voice on the council. Elod's medical training under a Tanis physician was cut short, which left him with the time to devote to the council. Plus, Reijo trusted him.

"*Khalon*...M'lady. I have to agree that something must be done for the missing women. I also understand that this is a time of great upheaval and that leaving the empire without the resources of the Tiaret warriors may be exactly what the enemy is hoping for with the continued attacks on our females, Earthling and Vukasin alike." Elod paused to gather his thoughts. "I suggest we do two things...for the remaining women, we should increase their protection. This should be done by the respective clans, which would eliminate any one clan being spread too thin."

Cais, the remaining Tanis council member, interrupted. "I agree with Elod that the women must be protected. But those of us who were once Tanis but remain loyal to the Ivailo line are too few to accomplish such a task. We are also particularly vulnerable because of our proximity to the Tanis desert stronghold, which is currently controlled by Bel's followers."

"It may be best if we relocate those women to other clans," one of the other council members suggested.

"No!" Cais almost came out of his chair. Megan

wasn't surprised at his outburst. Cais and Sara seemed to be getting along rather well. In fact, they seemed to be getting along about as well as her and Reijo were. It is doubtful either one would want to be away from the other.

Cais cleared his throat. "What I mean is our enemies would notice that something was amiss if we suddenly started moving all of the women. However, I believe they would expect all of the remaining Tanis to be under suspicion and wouldn't blink an eye at increased Empire troops in the area. I am asking for extra manpower to accomplish this."

"Fair enough." Ghaleb motioned to the scribe to make a note so troops could be assigned.

Megan knew that Elod knew one of the native women was reported missing because he was the one who had brought the missing natives to her attention. It didn't matter to her that the woman had been from the Tanis clan. She also knew him to be a fair and protective man. She waited patiently for him to bring up the other women. She knew that the men of the council would be more receptive to taking action if it came from one of their own. If Elod didn't speak up, then she would press the point.

Elod did not disappoint.

"As to the issue of the missing women, I agree that something must be done, not only because honor demands it of us because the women were under our protection but also because I believe that if we find the women we might find clues about the enemy's end game." Elod made sure that his eyes met the eyes of every council member. "With the glimpses I have had of the upper echelon of the Tanis clan, I seriously doubt that, when the war comes, it will be in a form that we are familiar with. The Tanis have primarily been about power, not honor…. Pardon for any insult, Cais."

"None taken."

"I suggest small investigative teams…two, maybe three people. They should not only be skilled trackers but men who would be able to plan and launch a rescue if the opportunity presented itself. Small teams would better be able to blend in and observe. Even if they don't locate the woman assigned to them, there is a good chance they could bring back information about our enemies."

Megan regarded Ghaleb. "Would that be acceptable to you?"

"I believe it is a fair compromise. And honestly it would probably be more effective than invading the Tanis stronghold. Don't you agree, Reijo?"

"Small teams make sense if we want to keep this as a covert operation. I will consult with the *kijani* from the various clans to recruit our best men."

"If we are all in agreement…." The council members confirmed their agreement. "I think we have accomplished enough for today, gentlemen…M'lady."

The members of the council as well as their guards filed out of the council chamber, the massive carved doors booming shut behind them. Megan stood and took Reijo's hand as they prepared to leave. The other council members had left, and the pair was almost to the door of the council chamber as well when Ghaleb called them back.

"Megan, Reijo…a moment if you don't mind."

Reijo and Megan followed the *Khalon* through the royal exit on the other side of the room. He led them back to the now familiar study where Ghaleb preferred to have conversations he would rather not be overheard.

Megan sat, but Reijo chose to remain standing behind her chair. Ghaleb leaned against his desk.

"You can come out now, Kavi."

A bent, white-haired man emerged from a hidden passageway. He kissed Megan's forehead by way of greeting before shaking Reijo's hand.

"Kavi, tell them what you told me."

Kavi slowly sank into a chair, looking for all the world like a decrepit old man. Reijo and Megan both knew that was a façade he cultivated to benefit his real position as Ghaleb's spy master.

Leaning back with a groan, Kavi said, "I believe I may have a lead on the Earth woman known as Maria Russo."

Ghaleb crossed his arms and caught Reijo's eye, "It's not quite as simple as Kavi says. There are a lot of rumors coming out of the desert. Something sinister is happening in the heart of Tanis territory. The Russo woman is only one piece of the puzzle." Ghaleb raised a hand, stopping Megan's protest. "Yes, I am concerned for her safety, and I also know that since she was supposed to go to one of the few Tanis households loyal to the Ivailo, that the clan presumably responsible for her won't have the resources to launch a rescue." Ghaleb rubbed tired eyes, "Knowing Megan, she will convince you to send a rescue party, Reijo."

Kavi took over the tale. "We have sent numerous spies into the area of the Tanis stronghold, but to date every single one has vanished or was a confirmed kill."

"Sounds like a traitor is in your midst."

Kavi nodded his head in agreement with Reijo. "More than one. At first these operations were approved by the council, so we assumed that a council member was possibly a traitor. We haven't been able to find proof of who that might be.

Unfortunately, when Ghaleb gave me the autonomy to not report to the council, our operatives were still being compromised. A systematic search has discovered a spy network to rival my own. We have interrogated and silenced at least half a dozen in the last two weeks alone. We believe we have turned a few of the traitor's operatives, but only time will tell how useful they will be."

"Why are you telling us this?" Megan asked.

"Because there is too much in the way of rumor coming from that stronghold, and we need some specific intel. Our current streams of information are suspect, and many of our men have not been re-vetted. We need eyes and ears we can trust implicitly. I want you to send Akia and Banji. Their eyes are dark enough that they won't be immediately recognized as Tiaret. Not only do we need the best—which we know they are—we also need a team we know we can trust without doubt. You have to admit, their loyalty is absolute."

"I don't really want to send those two. They are the core of the guards that I have watching over Megan and Abby."

I understand your position, Reijo," Ghaleb said, "but we need men we can trust, and those are few at the moment. I'm requesting this as your *Khalon.*"

"I'm assuming that on the surface this is to be

a rescue mission?" Reijo asked both Ghaleb and Kavi.

"If possible we would like them to head out without any word one way or the other. But, yes, if their mission comes to light, it will be simply played off as a rescue mission. But the primary objective would be to find out what in the twin moons is going on in the enemy camp."

CHAPTER THREE

Maria's head throbbed as she opened her eyes. Her vision blurred and the light was painful in her head. For a moment she couldn't understand why her heels were burning and her shoulder hurt. She then realized that she was being drug back to her cell by a hairy werewolf man. Evidently her captors got tired of her causing even minor injuries to their men when they came for her because today they sent a monster straight out of a horror movie.

At one point, Maria would have been terrified of the thing, but she had been on this planet long enough to discover the warriors had the capability of shifting into what they referred to as the phased state. It was their battle mode for lack of a better analogy. It made them stronger, faster, and tougher to kill, much like the mythological werewolf of Earth.

Maria twisted, trying to get out of the monster's grip only to have pain shoot through her abdomen. Those bastards had harvested her eggs without any anesthesia. Yes it was just giant needles piercing her midsection, but, damn it, those things hurt. She should have known that they were giving her hormone injections when they pulled her into the exam rooms, but life was so hellish she hadn't even considered that possibility. She had thought that they may be trying to get her pregnant with the number of times they had allowed her to be raped and the multiple medical exams. Evidently, she wasn't getting pregnant fast enough for their taste.

Mr. Hairy lifted her like she weighed nothing. Maria knew she still had ample curves despite the weight she had lost while in confinement. He flung her into her cell. Her back hit the stone wall, knocking the air from her lungs with a whoosh: more bruises to add to her growing collection. It was a miracle that every bone in her body wasn't broken.

Maria crawled to the far corner of her cell that she used as her bedroom. She closed her eyes and tried to recall Gio's face. Memories were the only good things she had left. It was getting harder and harder to bring to mind his easy going smile. She couldn't even remember if he had dimples or not. She should remember that kind of detail. She had told her grandfather that Gio was the love of her life. If he really was the love of her life, rape and torture shouldn't erase his face from her memory. Recently she wondered if she had fallen in love with the idea of Giovanni Luciano and not the actual man. Oh, she cared for him greatly, but she wasn't as sure of him as she had been the night she was taken. She wondered if she ever made it home if he would toss her aside as used. If they really had an epic love like she once asserted, she wouldn't have those kind of doubts. She would know that he would love her no matter what. She would know that he would wait for her. But even as her mind made those declarations, she knew that wouldn't be fair to Gio. By now she was most likely presumed dead and he was moving on with his life, as he should. It wasn't Gio's fault that she was here suffering alone.

Maria turned over to face the wall despite the discomfort it caused her battered body. She pushed her thick, matted, dark hair from her face as tears fells. She cried for *Nonno,* who would desperately search for his beloved granddaughter, only to never find her. She cried for the life that might have been and the pain that was. She cried until she fell into a troubled sleep.

*****

Screams woke Maria. At first she thought it was

the remnants of her horrible dreams, but her mind soon cleared enough for her to realize that the screams were coming from outside of her prison cell in the hallway. Maria got up and went to the door of her cell. She carefully lifted the small slit that the guards used to shove meager rations to her. She saw the guards dragging three new women.

The women looked similar to other new arrivals that had been coming in the past few days. They were small and delicate, even by human standards, which made them almost childlike by Vukasin standards. Maria would have thought them children if not for the lush curves on some and a few wrinkles found on others. They had almost a Polynesian appearance, but something was slightly off about their features…it was the eyes and proportions. Their eyes were large, giving them an almost doll-like appearance. Their eyes sparkled with an inner fire like a perfectly cut gemstone. Maria had never seen eyes like theirs.

Maria doubted they were from Earth. The women were pleading in a language that Maria didn't recognize, and she realized that these poor women didn't even have the benefit of the translator that Maria had had implanted in the imperial palace. They must be even more terrified than she had been.

Maria watched in horror as one of the women broke free and attacked the guards. She was desperately trying to free the other two women. Her meager strength was nothing more than an annoyance to the men manhandling them. A single blow to the side of the woman's head from the meaty fist of the guard had her staggering and dazed. One guard passed off the woman he was holding until only one of them held the other two women while his buddies held down and ripped at the third woman's clothing. She fought valiantly, but her meager strength was no match for two fully grown Vukasin men.

Even with her eyes closed, Maria could hear the screams and sobbing of the women. She owed it to them to see everything the Tanis inflicted upon them. She knew their pain, was their sister through shared experience. Knowing what was coming didn't make witnessing it any easier. She saw the vicious guard shove his swollen member into the tiny female without care for her discomfort. The blood on the poor girl's thighs was testament to the pain they caused.

Even with the knowledge that her struggles were futile, still the little woman fought back, clawing and tearing at the face and eyes of her attackers.

One guard grunted his finish and was shoved out of the way by the largest guard, who already had his pants around his ankles. He had been covetously stroking himself while the other guard sampled the poor woman first. The woman's fingernails found their target as the second man crawled on top of her, drawing blood from his face.

"You little whore!" he bellowed in fury and slapped her hard. Her head snapped back as he wrapped a large hand around the girl's delicate neck and he slammed into her over and over again.

Maria watched as the girl pulled at the guard's immovable fingers, trying to prevent them from squeezing the life from her. Her struggles were useless. Maria knew this and tears poured down her face as she watched in horror. The woman seemed so young, not much more than a child.

As the poor girl's lips turned blue, her attempts to free herself became weaker, until they ceased altogether. Her eyes stared accusingly and lifelessly at Maria as her tiny body continued to rock with the force of her murderer's thrusts. He hadn't even noticed she was dead until he finished.

"The boss isn't going to like the fact that you killed one of them, Krac," the guard who hadn't had a chance at the poor woman informed his cohort. His voice was hard and accusing, but Maria didn't mistake it for sympathy towards the dead girl. No, his disgust was simply at being denied his turn.

"Who gives dragon spider shit whether we break them or not. The village these breeders come from is riddled with so many women even the males just give them or sell them to us. The boss can always get more."

Krac stood and tossed the lifeless body at the remaining guard, a show of dominance. "Get rid of this while we put the others away."

Maria couldn't take being silent any longer. She started beating on her cell door and screaming. "She was a person! You can't just throw her away like trash!"

Krac turned toward Maria with a snarl. He phased into the monster that had hauled Maria back to her cell earlier. Watching the man turn into a monster had the women screaming anew. Maria just glared at him. At this point she had seen it all and didn't give a shit that he was trying to intimidate her as he disengaged the locks.

Somewhere in the back of her mind she knew this could be the cause of her death, but it took too much energy to work up caring. Maria knew he was trying to scare her, but she didn't have any fear left in her at this point. She wasn't afraid of pain or death. She had reached her limit. Dying would almost be easier. At least then she wouldn't have to suffer any more.

Just as that thought slipped through her mind, her heart rejected it. As long as she was still alive, there was still hope. Yet she couldn't make herself back down and retreat. She would never allow them to break her.

Maria's eyes flashed with renewed fire. "You heard me, you mangy mutt! She was a living being and she deserves your respect!"

Krac threw open her cell door and grabbed Maria by her long thick hair before she could duck away from his grasp. One hand pulled her into the air by her hair while the other grasped Maria's neck and squeezed. Her feet dangled in the air, not giving her any purchase to leverage her way out of Krac's grasp. She knew she couldn't pull his fingers from her neck, so she did the only thing she could think of; she slammed her knee into his nose. A small trickle of blood was her only reward. She just didn't have the power needed to make the move more than an annoyance. Krac squeezed her neck tighter, cutting Maria's air off completely.

Maria refused to look away from the creature that was killing her. She could see the pleasure he derived from inflicting pain and death in his eyes. Even as the darkness crept through the edge of her vision, she glared at him.

"Krac, put her down. You have cost me enough today with your careless actions." Maria could hear the cultured tones of the man she had begun to refer to as 'the Doctor' because she had only ever seen him in the examination rooms before today. While taller than many humans, he was a slight man by

Vukasin standards. His temple was frosted with grey, and wrinkles could be seen around his eyes. While not a young man, it was impossible to guess at the Doctor's age.

Maria dropped to the floor, gasping for air. She turned her head so she could see the Doctor through the fall of her hair. Krac returned to his human-looking form and bowed his head, bearing his neck like a dog facing the alpha male of a pack. It continued to surprise Maria that the muscle-bound Krac showed so much deference to the physically weaker Doctor. It made her wonder just what the man had on his guards because they didn't follow him out of a sense of loyalty as far as she could tell. Somehow the Doctor was the more powerful male, and that fact scared her more than Krac's muscle-bound threats.

"Get the new arrivals into their cells. We have work to do." The Doctor turned and nearly ran into the thin man who brought the captives their food. The man cowered as the Doctor shooed him away.

Krac once again grabbed Maria by her hair and tossed her into her cell, slamming the door shut. Maria could hear him bellowing at the other guards as they moved away from her cell.

Maria clutched her aching head. Her mother had always told her that she needed to learn when to keep her mouth shut. At the moment, Maria had to agree with her dearly departed mother. Her outburst had changed nothing, except she had an even bigger headache and more bruises. Tears shimmered in Maria's eyes. She dashed them away quickly. If she started crying now she wasn't sure she would be able to stop.

Her situation felt hopeless. Maria did what she always did when she felt no hope; she prayed for a miracle. Back home she prayed for her patients; today she prayed for herself. She knew if nothing else changed she was going to die in this miserable place. Despite her situation, she wasn't quite ready to give up just yet.

Her food came sliding through the slot on a metal tray. Maria rubbed her throat. It was doubtful she could eat without pain. She could still feel Krac's hand on her neck squeezing the life from her. He had been so much stronger than she was. Nothing she could do would change the fact that because she was weaker, she was at the mercy of the strong. It wasn't fair.

In a pique of rage, Maria picked up the metal tray of food and hurled it into the wall. It gave a satisfying crash. But when she saw the food scattered all around, she started to cry despite her best efforts not to. Maria then slumped down onto the floor to hug her knees.

Maria let her despair weigh her down for a little

bit before her practical nature kicked back in again. She crawled over to where the food lay on the dirt floor. Even if she couldn't eat it now, she would need it for later. She knew she had to keep her strength up. She might not be able to fight the guards, but that didn't mean that she might not find an opportunity to escape. She reached for the metal tray, intending to put the food back on it.

"Ouch," Maria saw a trickle of blood at the tip of her finger, like she had a really bad paper cut. When Maria flipped the tray over, she found that her tray had knocked a shard of the stone wall off. It was about the size of her palm and the edge was razor sharp. As weapons go it wasn't much, but it gave her hope. It also gave her an idea.

She pulled the tangled mess of her long, dark hair over her shoulder. *Nonno* had always said that a woman's hair was her crowning glory. So it didn't surprise Maria when she started to cry as she hacked the long locks as short as she could manage with her stone knife. She could almost hear her grandfather's voice admonishing her for ruining her beautiful hair. Even Gio had loved her long hair, but Gio and *Nonno* weren't there. Krac was.

Maria vowed she wasn't going to give Krac the opportunity to use her hair to subdue her again. She also promised to use her stone knife to gut him if the opportunity presented itself. What's one more sin to add to her stained soul?

CHAPTER FOUR

"Gods forsaken sand fleas!" Banji slapped at his neck and scowled at his stoic brother. "Why are we in this dust bowl again? And why aren't these damned bugs not biting you?" The only change in Akia's expression was the lifting of a single brow. If they weren't on a mission, Banji would punch his brother just to get a reaction out of the man.

The pair was crammed into the dusty corner of a questionable tavern. They had abandoned their uniforms for mismatched armor and weapons. To a stranger they looked like any number of nomadic mercenaries that traveled through El-Bahar, the Tanis capitol city.

Despite the arid climate, the Tanis clan had made El-Bahar a thriving metropolis with their use of research and science. Of course it was said that the Tanis greed in exploiting the local resources for science had left the once lush area in the desert state it was now in. In fact, the Tanis example was often cited as the reason for the decisions the ruling body made to preserve ecology over "progress."

Even with limited vegetation and water resources, Tanis maintained its position of power through its mineral resources and scientific discoveries. Unfortunately not everyone within the clan benefited equally. Unlike the Tiaret who stressed working together to achieve a goal, the Tanis believed strongly in survival of the fittest. You can't have large populations of people without the seedy underbelly of society popping up somewhere. In El-Bahar, seedy was the normal. Everyone plotted and scraped just to survive. Only the most dangerous thrived here.

"Are you sure about this contact, Akia?"

Akia lifted his drink. Banji noticed that his brother didn't swallow. So Akia had the same bad vibe that Banji did. The act of drinking put the people around them at ease. Not actually ingesting the potent alcohol kept the brothers' wits sharp.

People stared whenever they were together. Twins were extremely rare on Vukas. Identical twins were unheard of. In fact few people outside of Ghaleb and Reijo's inner circle knew the twins existed. It was one of the reasons Kavi had recruited them.

It unnerved many to see such exact copies

side by side, which was why they kept their cloaks up to hide their faces. They had the height most Vukasin people seemed to have. Their hair was dark and a bit on the shaggy side. Banji and Akia were mirror images. One drank with his left hand, the other his right, but few noticed such little details.

With the exception of a few romps at the pleasure houses, they rarely appeared in public together. When sent on most assignments people assumed that there was only one person. Often one would be seen publicly while the other did the retrieval or reconnaissance. The public brother always had a rock solid alibi, even if the other happened to be seen. Unfortunately this assignment wasn't infiltrating posh homes in search of political spies. In this assignment, their unique looks seemed to be more of a determent than an asset; almost every eye in the tavern had stared and whispered, even with the cover of the shadows. They had done their best to minimize their looks. Each dressed very differently. Akia had cut his hair short while Banji left it long. But their voices, faces and mannerisms weren't so easy to hide.

"Kavi said that this man had passed along information that strange women were being transported through this area." Akia looked around the tavern. Their contact was late, and that never boded well.

"Women of any sort would draw attention these days. Are we sure they weren't just Tanis females being brought to their capitol because of the threat of war?"

"According to the description it was fairly obvious that these were not Vukasin females." Akia looked up towards the door.

The dim space brightened as several men entered. Akia and Banji were concealed under hooded cloaks in the shadows, and both pulled the hood of their cloak lower. The man who appeared to be the leader turned to the tavern owner. A serpent crest flashed in the light of the closing door. What were Tanis soldiers doing here? Their contact had chosen this tavern because it was in an area that the soldiers rarely dared to venture. It was known that the men who lived in this part of El-Bahar would slit your throat for the slightest reason; some did it just for fun.

The tavern owner first shook his head until the soldier grabbed his head and slammed it into the bar top. It was a testament to the daily violence the tavern patrons endured when not a single one voiced outrage or leapt to the owner's defense. With his faced pushed down and bleeding, the owner waved a shaky finger in the general direction of Banji and Akia.

"Brother, I think we are about to have

trouble." Akia stood, pulling his gun from its holster, hiding it in the folds of his cloak. He was trying to form a plan to extract them from this situation without drawing undue attention. Unfortunately, Banji had other ideas.

Banji grinned and unsheathed his blade. "This isn't trouble...this is fun." Without giving his brother a chance to protest, Banji launched himself onto a nearby table. Using the table tops, he rushed the soldiers at the door, knocking two of the four out into the courtyard.

The tavern was frozen in shock before erupting into pandemonium. All it took to set off a chain of violence was a single person to start brawling. The tavern's customers started attacking anyone near them: friend...foe...it didn't seem to matter. The patrons caught a third soldier in the midst of their brawl.

Akia sighed and made his way to the door to fetch his brother. Once again he was going to have to save his brother's backside. He side-stepped and turned, avoiding the majority of the chaos in a warrior's dance. Akia had never really been one for close-quarters combat like his brother. He'd much rather pick off his targets at a distance—less messy.

Akia had his hand on the door of the tavern when a massive hand grabbed his shoulder. Akia elbowed the solar plexus of the man who grabbed him and turned to face his opponent in what appeared to be a single move.

The leader of the Tanis soldiers wheezed as he stood up, drawing his sword. "You are under arrest."

"On who's authority?"

"By the authority of the *Khalon* of the true imperial family, Bel of Tanis."

Akia smiled a feral smile. "He's no *Khalon* of mine."

"Good. Now I can have some fun." The soldier moved into a battle stance, his left sword arm raised high. Akia's eyes were drawn to a brand on the soldiers forearm. It was large and looked like a serpent eating its own tail. Tattoos and branding were practices that were given up in antiquity on Vukas, so it shocked him to see one on the traitorous soldier.

Akia raised his gun to finish off the last soldier in the tavern when the man exploded into action. He should have still been winded with the blow that Akia had given him, allowing the Tiaret to finish him off quickly. The Tanis soldier recovered abnormally fast.

The soldier knocked Akia's gun from his hand with a slap of the wrist, radiating pain up Akia's arm. The strength of the attack surprised Akia. The man was large like all Vukasin warriors, but the power behind his blows seemed disproportionate to his size. Something strange was going on here.

"What in the five hells...." The slice of his attacker's blade across his bicep pushed the mystery to the back of his mind. Akia sank into the pool of calm and allowed his warrior's training to take over. No one was better trained than the Tiaret warriors. His focused on the battle at hand: pain, distraction, fear...all of it was locked away until only battle strategy remained.

Akia traded blows with his attacker, barely missing anything vital being skewered by the sword. The rapid assault kept him on the defensive, but even as he retreated, his mind was watching for patterns in the Tanis soldier's attack. If he could see the pattern, he might—*Ah ha! There it is, an opening.* It was small but it was there. The soldier favored the same sweeping pattern with his sword, a figure eight slashing across the body. When he shifted his arm to move into a thrust instead of a slash, for a brief moment he left his body open.

Akia fell and rolled away from the Tanis soldier. He palmed the dagger he kept in his boot as he rolled. He jumped up, dagger in hand and braced himself. His back was against the door, so he would only have one chance. He found his chance when the Tanis came at him with the slash and thrust pattern

Akia had noticed.

"Today you die, Spy!"

The Tanis soldier prepared to thrust his sword into Akia's gut. Akia spun, letting the blade graze his side so he could bury his dagger in between his attacker's ribs and up into his heart.

The Tanis's eyes flew open and he tried to speak as blood foamed up in his mouth. Akia had shredded his lung as well as his heart. He watched as the life left the soldier's eyes and he sank to the ground, blood pooling around him.

"Not today, Tanis!"

When the Tanis soldier was dead, Akia removed his dagger, wiping the blood on the dead man's shirt. He stood and kicked open the door, rushing through to find his brother.

Banji was bloodied, kneeling on the ground surrounded by an entire squadron of Tanis soldiers. He smiled at Akia, wincing as his split lip started bleeding again, and shrugged.

"By the moons…it just might be today."

CHAPTER FIVE

Voices and the metallic slamming of the door at the end of the hall woke Maria. She quickly moved to the door to see what she could spy through the small hatch. The Doctor's goons were dragging what appeared to be a couple of unconscious men. These men didn't appear to be the obviously poor and downtrodden that the Doctor had collected for experiments, and they didn't wear the uniforms of the other guards, so that eliminated them being a guard who had displeased one of the higher ups. These men looked like they could be elite soldiers just about anywhere. They were very well muscled, even in their relaxed state.

The guards threw one man into the open cell and slammed the door shut. They then went down the line trying to find a cell for the second man, but all of them were packed to the brim with the exotic women brought in. Her cell had been the only one with a single occupant. The empty cell had only been emptied that morning. The poor women never seemed to return when they left here. Maria wondered if they were strong enough to survive the experimentation she had endured since they seemed so fragile. The women rapidly dying would explain their disappearance.

"Damn the moons, they are all full. What in the five hells are we supposed to do with this guy? Krac said the *kijani* wanted them separated before the interrogator got here."

"Stick him in the Earth woman's cell. There is still room in there."

"I'm not sure the researchers would like that. They want her kept isolated. That's one of the reasons we haven't put any of the village females with her."

"I take my orders from my *kijani,* not from some feeble scientist. He wants the men separated. Besides, it's not like they will be here very long anyway."

"You better sign off on this because I've seen what happens when you get on the bad side of that 'feeble' scientist. I want no part of that."

"Whatever, let's just get this done. It's time for my midday meal."

Maria scurried from the door as the guard laid his palm on the console to open it. She was sore enough that she didn't need to add anymore bruises from being kicked out of the way. In her sleeping corner she grasped the stone shard and hid it behind her back. The guards tossed the newcomer in and slammed the door, once more engaging the locks.

*****

Maria crouched in her sleeping corner, her grip on the sharp stone cutting into her palm. Was the man being put in her cell really just a coincidence or was this another sick experiment? She wouldn't put it past the Doctor to see how she would react to a male prisoner instead of a guard, which was why she vowed to stay as far away from the newcomer as the confines of her cell would allow her to.

Time passed. Maria wasn't sure how long she crouched in her corner, but the shadows from her single window had lengthened, so the day was almost over. Still the man didn't move. She studied him from a distance. His battered face testified to the brawl that took him out. He obviously didn't go quietly. She had seen her fair share of faces distorted by trauma, and she could tell that when healed her new roommate would be a handsome man.

Maria inched closer, even as she berated herself. The fact that the man hadn't stirred concerned her. Despite her misgivings, the nurse in her couldn't resist the need to help. Reaching down, she was relieved to find a strong pulse on his wrist. She walked around his body. She couldn't really see his injuries under his shirt, but a bloody gash on the side of the head gave a pretty strong clue to what knocked him out.

She knelt down to feel around the man's scalp for fractures when a deep voice yelled out from the other cell.

"Hey! Where's my brother!"

Clang of metal echoed across the hall. The newest prisoner beat on the cell door as if he was trying to break it down. Maria could have told him that it wouldn't work. Other men had tried the same thing; none of them succeeded in even denting the door.

The loud noise had the poor women wailing. Maria knew it had to be terrifying not being able to understand the language surrounding them. The newcomer's yells most likely sounded threatening to them. The man in the other cell must have heard them because he gentled his voice and started asking the other women if they knew anything about his brother. The fact that he spoke to the women in calming tones didn't go unnoticed by Maria. Either he was a good actor or the prisoner was a better man than the guards they dealt with daily. She decided to take a chance that he might be what he seemed.

"They can't understand you," Maria called.

She moved over to the door to better communicate. "As far as I can tell, those terrified women weren't given the translation implant."

"Are you Vukasin?"

"No, I'm from Earth." Maria thought for a moment. "I don't think I have seen them bring in Vukasin women."

"You wouldn't happen to be Maria Russo would you?"

Maria took an involuntary step back from the door. She hadn't heard her own name in months. She was just 'the subject' when the Doctor was referring to her, and the guards called her whore. "H...How do you know my name?"

"Well at least this little misadventure wasn't a total loss. Eh, Akia?"

Maria whipped around at the amused masculine voice behind her. She screamed as she fell back against the door, raising her hands for an attack. Thankfully she kept ahold of her stone knife. The large man they threw in her cell had woken up while she talked to the other and was now standing in the middle of the cell, which didn't seem small until his presence filled it. She brandished her makeshift knife in front of her, squeezing the stone until blood ran from her palm.

"Banji, what's going on?"

Banji approached Maria with both palms up.

"I mean you no harm, M'lady." He called out to his brother. "It's fine. I just startled the lady."

"Don't let my oaf of a brother frighten you, though his face could scare small children." The man in her cell let out a deep rumbling laugh after that statement.

Maria retreated as far as she could as the man called Banji moved towards her, but she had to fight not to smile at his brother's jab. She had to remind herself that this could still be a cruel experiment.

"Who are you?"

"Why, we are here to rescue you."

CHAPTER SIX

Banji had woken up when her small fingers had gingerly probed his head for injury. He had lain there quietly and observed her through veiled eyes. She was beautiful even in her unwashed state, and not just physically, though the short halo of curly dark hair surrounding her heart-shaped face and deep golden eyes would definitely grab a man's attention. She was kind and compassionate. Her body trembled in terror, yet she still gently assessed the wounds of a stranger thrown in with her. She called out to reassure his brother. Yes, she held much compassion in her heart.

While her back was still turned, Banji stood up and made his presence known. He almost wished he hadn't as Maria fell against the door hard enough to add yet another bruise to her battered body.

Now that Banji was standing with wide open eyes, he could see the full extent of how badly this gentle woman had been used. The injuries that marred her skin made him want to howl in rage, but he kept tight control on his emotions because he despised the look of stark terror in her eyes. But even in her terror she was a fighter and resourceful, as evidenced by the makeshift weapon she held. She obviously did not have the warrior's training that Megan had. She was sitting on the ground; he could have easily subdued her by force. But she held the stone knife in front of her, the edge sharp enough to cause her to bleed as she gripped it tightly. She ignored the pain, keeping her weapon between him and her.

When he announced that he and Akia were her rescuers, she snorted a laugh, which made him grin. The Tanis hadn't broken her spirit if she was willing to call into question the word of a man twice her size. And Banji had to admit that if he was in her place he would question the validity of the statement as well.

"Granted it appears we aren't doing a very good job, but I assure you that my brother and I have gotten out of worse situations." Banji noticed blood seeping between the fingers wrapped around her stone shard and sliding down her forearm. With a muttered curse, he quickly moved to grab her hands.

Maria gasped at his quick movements and struggled to try and free herself from his grip. She knew she shouldn't have let her guard down. Once again she would be injured by a man larger than she simply because he was physically stronger.

His large hand easily held her wrists like an iron vice. She twisted and pulled, but his hand never tightened. Despite his immovable grip, he was careful not to crush or bruise her. Maria frowned as he turned her hand to examine it. She tried once more to get him to let her go.

"Be calm, M'lady." He pried her fingers apart and removed the stone shard. Maria couldn't suppress the hiss of pain as the sharp edge was removed from the flesh of her palm. The man muttered soothing nonsense like she was an injured child. He tried to wipe away the blood with one hand, but it had little effect. Muttering a curse, he finally released her hand.

Banji tore off a sleeve of his shirt and looked around the sparse cell. He found the metal flask that the guards gave them for water. He lifted it and frowned at how little water was inside. Instead of soaking the makeshift rag like he would have preferred, he just dabbed enough to make it slightly damp. He returned to Maria much more slowly than when he first reached for her. She eyed him like the dog deer when cornered by a ghost lion. If he had his way, he would kill every male that put that fear into her eyes.

He crouched down near her and held out his hand. Everything in him wanted to snatch it quickly and treat her wounds, but he didn't want to cause her anymore fear. His open palm hovered in the air and he was worried that perhaps it was too much asking her to trust him with touching her. He gazed at Maria's face and held her eyes. A slight nod towards his outstretched hand was all he gave as a request. Gingerly, Maria lifted her shaking hand and laid it in his open palm. Gently he took her hand in his and cleaned away the blood from the cut on her palm. It was such a small thing to be allowed to treat her wounds, but in that moment it felt like she had given him the world.

"Who are you?" Maria searched Banji's face. He didn't have the same cruelness the guards had in their eyes. He was most assuredly not the unemotional robot she saw in the Doctor. She wasn't foolish enough to think this man wasn't deadly. The way he moved screamed warrior.

Banji wrapped her hand in another strip torn from his shirt and sat back. He smiled at her, and she could tell from the creases around his mouth that he smiled often. It made her want to smile in return.

"I'm Banji of the clan—"

Maria launched herself at him, covering his mouth quickly. "Shhh…the walls have ears and eyes." She didn't want him to reveal his clan because she knew that the Tanis would seek vengeance for any perceived slight. Even if Banji and Akia were to die in this prison, the Tanis clan would target their friends and family.

Banji nodded his head to let Maria know that he understood. He went to the door and called out to his brother. To Maria, it sounded like gibberish and her translator refused to translate, much like it had with the other women's language. So whatever language the brothers were speaking it wasn't known to the technology implanted in her brain.

All twins create their own language. Most grow out of its use as they age, but Akia and Banji kept their secret language going for their entire lives. It was a unique set of phonics and even a bit of telepathy. In the heat of battle it allowed them to call out maneuvers without the enemy knowing what they were about to do. Banji used that language now.

"Akia, do you still have your tool kit?"

"Yes, why?"

"Maria is certain that the cells are monitored, though at first glance I can't see anything."

"You know that doesn't mean anything, Banji. She has been here much longer than we have. If she thinks the cells are being monitored she probably has a reason for it."

"Well what can you do about it?"

"Kavi gave me one of those crystals that let you know if there is a monitoring device in the vicinity. Give me a minute and I will let you know if any are in my cell for certain." Akia pulled a special thread in his pants. It unraveled to reveal a hidden pocket. With movements trained not to draw attention, Akia pulled a small crystal, which was glowing red, an indication that a covert listening device was nearby. He paced around his cell waiting for the device to turn yellow. It turned yellow in the far corner.

Akia made a show of looking over the cell as if seeking a way out. It was normal for prisoners to inspect their cells after being confined. Akia used that to conceal the fact that he was looking for something specific. After a careful search, Akia found a small listening device and crystal camera hidden in a small crevice in the stone wall. He passed over the devices as if he hadn't discovered them and continued his 'search' for a way out.

He returned to the door and called to his brother. *"Banji, audio and visual monitoring in my cell. Which means there is probably the same in yours."*

Banji paced and switched to telepathy. Language patterns could always be cracked, but no one would know if he silently spoke to his brother's mind.

Damn it to the five hells! How are we going to get Maria out of here without alerting the whole place? Hells, we don't even know for certain where we are at ourselves.

Be calm brother and give me a chance to think.

"I know you were talking about me; for some reason the translator couldn't figure out what the hell you were saying, but I heard my name." Maria crossed her arms and glared at Banji.

Banji moved over and wrapped her in his arms. Maria stiffened, not expecting to be held in his encompassing embrace. She wasn't a petite woman, at least by Earth standards; she was just a few inches shy of six foot tall. Yet, her head barely reached Banji's shoulder. Soon she found herself melting into Banji's warmth. It had been a long time since anyone held her to try and comfort her.

Banji leaned his head down, his breath whispering across Maria's ear. "My brother is trying to figure out a way to get us out of here. He confirmed we are being monitored both in audio and visual, which complicates matters."

Maria leaned her head against Banji's forehead. She cupped his cheeks with her hands, playing along with the comforting embrace, while obscuring her mouth from outside eyes. "How are you going to get all of these women out of here?"

"I'm sorry, Maria. You are our priority. We don't have the resources to take the rest of the women with us. I promise that once you are safe we will have a squadron here to get the rest of the women," Banji whispered.

Maria shoved away from him and stalked to the other side of the cell, the need for discretion forgotten in her anger. "That's not good enough, Banji. You don't know what they have done in here…. I do."

CHAPTER SEVEN

Banji doubted that Maria would be able to tell them any great mysteries of their prison, but she might give him a detail that they could use. If nothing else, he was certain that getting her talking would give him a better chance of having her back in his arms, a goal he suddenly found very important.

"Tell me what you know." Banji sat down in the middle of the cell and motioned Maria to come closer.

He and his brother were going to be lucky to get themselves and Maria out of this prison; there was just no way they could take any of the other women. The sheer numbers would have made that difficult, but couple that with the women being unable to understand them and it would make an impromptu rescue attempt impossible.

Banji was an honorable man and he wouldn't promise something he knew he could not do. He hated that he would be unable to give in to Maria's demands because he would like nothing more than to rescue every woman held here. But he also knew that they had a better chance of saving them if they only took Maria and returned at a later date with more men. He needed to distract Maria from that fact, but he also needed to know what kind of information she could give them.

Maria looked around nervously and hedged, "I'm fairly certain someone watches us all of the time."

That was a given after finding the monitoring devices. But he needed to keep her talking, so Banji played along, "What makes you say that?"

"They always seem to know what is going on down here." Maria hugged her arms close to her chest. It always amazed her how some memories could hurt physically. "There is this guard...I heard the others call him Krac. He's brutal...seems to enjoy dealing out pain. The other day they brought in some more of the strange women. One managed to break away and tried to escape. They caught her and started to rape her, forcing the others to watch. When Krac had his turn she was able to claw at his eyes...."

Banji was fascinated at the way Maria talked with her hands. Her entire body was so expressive. She didn't have to say anything as her voice trailed off. Her face paled and her entire body shuddered as if it was about to be sick.

"You don't have to tell me if it is too painful."

Maria shook her head. "Someone needs to know…*madre di dio*. I watched them throw her away like trash." Banji surmised that the poor girl hadn't survived the incident. He kept quiet for fear that the rage simmering within would frighten Maria.

Maria took a steadying breath. "Before Krac had been able to pull his pants back up the Doctor came in to chastise him. He never comes down here, but he knew what had happened. Someone had to have told him, or he had to have seen it himself."

"Which confirmed that they monitored this area for you? But now we were able to give you proof." Maria nodded. "Who is this doctor?"

Maria slid to the floor and hugged her knees; her eyes looked haunted. "I don't know his name. Up until he came down here that one time, I had only ever seen him in the examination room."

Maria wouldn't look at him. Whatever had happened in the examination room had caused her shame. "Maria, can you continue? Or should we stop for now?"

Banji wanted to know what the doctor had done, if for no other reason so that he could repay the man tenfold for the pain he had caused Maria. As much as he desired to know, if Maria didn't want to continue, he would stop. He wasn't going to add to her trauma, especially since he knew that the truth of what had happened to her would eventually come to light when he got her back to a medical facility.

Blinking back tears, Maria took a deep breath. "He seems to be conducting both a breeding program and experiments. They brought in various men; most seemed like the type that wouldn't be missed...criminals, the homeless. Every once in a while a guard who had displeased someone was thrown in. When those men were taken to the exam rooms, you never saw them again, but sometimes the screams reached even here."

"What happened to you?" Banji couldn't stop himself from asking. He wanted to know everything about Maria, even the ugly things. He knew that the Tanis had had Maria for months. He also knew from Maria's tone that what Krac had done to the other woman wasn't an unusual occurrence. Banji knew trained warriors that would have fallen apart under that kind of stress for that length of time. For Maria to have survived so long....

Maria sobbed, but shook her head. She couldn't tell him what they had done to her. She didn't want to remember what they had done to her. If he made her face it all right now, she would shatter.

Banji's heart broke. Maria had retreated into herself. He could almost see the wall she erected in her mind. What kind of monsters were they dealing with? Despite his pounding head, Banji called to his brother via their telepathic link, even as he moved to comfort Maria with his embrace.

Akia, how could they break something so beautiful and good?

"Shhh, little one…as long as I breathe they won't harm you again."

She's not broken, Banji. In pain, yes. Broken, no. If she was broken she wouldn't have tried to still fight you.

Banji considered his brother's words. Maria wasn't trained to fight, and she had suffered much, but even now she had challenged Banji, a man twice her size and strength, with nothing but a piece of stone. Her heart may be soft and bruised, but her will was as strong as Vukasin steel. It shamed him that even for a moment he thought of her as broken.

I suppose you are right, brother. But what do we do now? I feel such a protective streak for her. It doesn't feel normal.

I wouldn't worry about it. I can see in your mind that she is a beautiful woman, and she is obviously compassionate. Any honorable warrior would feel the need to protect her. Rest. I can feel your pain.

Akia severed their connection. Banji knew as far as he was concerned the matter was over, but he wasn't so sure. He was drawn to Maria in a way that he had never been drawn to anyone before—not even with Abby, Megan's small daughter, had Banji felt this demand to be with her and protect her always.

Banji looked down at the woman wrapped in his arms. Her sobs had quieted and he found she had fallen into an exhausted sleep. His shirt was damp with her tears, but he didn't care.

He reached up and gently moved the short curls from her face. Her hair wound around his fingers, as if willing him to stay. The short strands fascinated him. They were dark like a Vukasin but with shots of a warm amber color throughout. She was so different from the brassy fire of Megan and Abby. Banji discovered he preferred Maria's softer looks. He wondered if her hair would still call to him after years together.

What in the five hells am I thinking? He had no right to think about a future with Maria. As much as he suddenly found himself craving the idea of them being together, he couldn't ask that of her. She had endured so much already. No, it was better that he act as her protector. He would prevent anything else from harming her, even if it cost him his life. In that way he could say that he had a small part in any future happiness and in the meantime he could bask in whatever gentle kindness she chose to give him.

Banji spotted the thin blanket in the corner. Gently, he picked up the sleeping Maria and moved her to her sleeping corner. She whimpered in her sleep and clung to him when he tried to move away. He feared waking her, so instead he lay down next to her. The warrior pillowed her head against his chest, making sure that his body stood between her and the cell door. He had no idea when someone would come into the cell, but he would stand between her and whatever came through that door.

It didn't take long for Banji to succumb to his own exhaustion. There was an old adage in the warrior's circles, "Sleep when you can, but sleep light." Banji might as well get what rest he could. Closing his eyes, he drifted away, dreaming of a beautiful woman with golden eyes.

CHAPTER EIGHT

Banji…Banji…wake up you son of a….

Do not disparage our mother, Akia.

Banji rubbed the dryness from his eyes. His right side was unusually warm. Then he remembered the beautiful woman curled up next to him. Maria had thrown a leg over Banji's hips. Her head was still tucked onto his shoulder, her breath warm against his chest. They may be in a prison cell, but this felt right. What would it be like to wake every morning like this?

Banji grinned.

You can drop the smugness. We've got to get out of here.

Maria is coming with us.

Of course she is. Banji could hear the impatience in his brother's mind. *She was our primary objective as far as Megan and Reijo were concerned.*

She doesn't want to leave the other women.

She won't have a choice, Akia's voice barked in Banji's mind.

What has happened? You are not usually this cranky in the morning.

I overheard the guards as they made the morning rounds. We are going to be interrogated.

And? The brothers had been trained to withstand many forms of interrogation, including torture.

They were taking bets on how long we would survive the questioning by Sta'ling Tanis.

It can't be him. The Butcher was imprisoned and slated for execution because of his gruesome experiments.

The thought that Sta'ling "The Butcher" Tanis roamed free chilled Banji to the bone. He had been on the team sent to arrest the man and he still had nightmares about what he saw. The man was obsessed with making predators, including men, more dangerous. In his pursuit of that end, he had earned the butcher title because one of his primary lines of experimentation was to see how much pain and suffering a subject could endure before dying or turning into a mindless monster. Banji helped free one of Sta'ling's subjects. The man had been filleted alive. His voice begging Banji to kill him echoed though his memories.

Don't you ever pay attention when we are at

the war briefings? Akia got his brother's attention once more, dragging him out of the dark past.

That's what I have you for. You are the brains of our outfit; I'm just the good looks.

Akia tried to suppress a smile. After all they were identical twins. It amazed him how Banji could keep his good humor in the most dire of circumstances.

Well, to refresh your memory, Sta'ling's prison was one of the first raids the Tanis conducted. Kavi was fairly certain the goal had been the Butcher's release. He was one of Bel's right hand men after all.

Banji thought of an Earth saying that Megan was fond of repeating: "Hindsight is 20/20." When he looked back now he could clearly see the clues of the rotting evil that pervaded the upper echelon of the Tanis Clan. Little good it did them in their current situation.

So what's the plan?

Do you have that little device Kavi gave us to disrupt monitoring devices?

Yeah, it was sewn into my pant leg.

I'm going to modify the frequency on mine so that it opens the crystal locks.

These are DNA locks, Akia, and we don't have time to try and get a guard's DNA. You can't just zap it with an energy blast.

One of Kavi's techs figured out that you could overload the DNA locking mechanism by downloading massive amounts of information. I'm modifying the frequency to mimic multiple downloads. In theory it should work. That will leave yours for turning the eyes and ears off for a while.

What are we going to do after that?

I have no frexing clue. We were both unconscious when we were brought in her, so I suppose we will get out of here "by the seat of our pants" as Megan would say.

Banji laughed out loud. *You without a plan...this should be interesting.*

*****

Maria woke up warm. She and Gio must have fallen asleep on the couch again. She stretched and trailed her hand down Gio's chest. Her brow scrunched...that didn't feel like Gio's chest and abs. Gio worked in an office; while not overweight, he was soft, not the rock hard muscles she had under her hands. Maybe she was still dreaming.

Suddenly reality came crashing down on her. She wasn't back in Italy. This wasn't her apartment. She had been kidnapped and was in a cell on some foreign planet. She bolted upright. *Madre dios, I slept with an alien.* She pinched the bridge of her nose and groaned.

"Are you alright, Maria?" Banji's deep rumbling voice sent shivers down her spine.

Maria sighed. She tried once again to recall Giovanni's face and voice. But at best it was a hazy recollection. She could still clearly picture her *nonno*. Maybe her experiences in this hell had made it so she wouldn't be able to be attracted to a man. Perhaps that is why she couldn't really picture her former fiancé's face clearly.

Banji sat up and rubbed his rough hands up and down Maria's arms. She knew that he could tell something was bothering her and was trying to comfort her, but his gentle actions felt more erotic than comforting to her. It had been a long time since she felt like someone cared for her. She couldn't really use the argument that she was unable to feel attraction to a man after the horrors she had suffered when her body heated up at the touch of Banji's hands, all of which just made her feel even worse.

Disgusted with herself, Maria quickly stood up and marched across the cell to the bucket that she used as a chamber pot. She skidded to a halt when she realized that there wasn't any privacy to take care of her morning business. Damn it! Her bladder was crying for her to go relieve it, but she just couldn't bring herself to pee in front of a stranger.

Banji must have noticed Maria fidgeting and realized what the issue was.

"I'll give you some privacy," Banji said while turning around. The maneuver was rather pointless since Maria now knew that they were being filmed. But some faceless man behind a monitor was easier to block out when her bladder was screaming than a living, virile male in front of her eyes.

Maria relieved herself as quickly as possible.

"My turn." Banji jumped up when Maria returned to the sleeping corner. "Of course, I'm not quite as shy. Feel free to look if you want," Banji winked as he walked past.

Red crept up Maria's cheeks until her face was burning with embarrassment.

"I can't believe you said that!" She whipped around to chastise him only to catch Banji with his pants down, literally. She couldn't see his front, but his backside was definitely nice...better than nice. It was the kind of ass that made a woman want to grab it and hold on for the ride. *Dio!* Where the hell had that thought come from? She turned her back to him and hung her head in her hands with a groan.

She could hear Banji's chuckle over the sounds of his morning relief.

CHAPTER NINE

Banji loved teasing Maria. She blushed so beautifully. Despite the abuse she had sustained, she somehow managed to keep a certain innocence about her. There was a quiet strength in being able to remain innocent in the midst of horror.

As much as he would love to bask in the glow of small moments, time was running short.

Keeping his back to the hidden monitoring device, Banji wrapped Maria in his arms from behind. If a guard was watching, it would look like he was putting the moves on the woman he shared a cell with. Since women were in such short supply, no one would question a man trying to take advantage of proximity.

Banji leaned down. Maria could feel his warm breath on her ear, "If we can get the doors open can you lead us out of here?"

Maria shook her head. "No, I was

unconscious when they brought me here. All I know is this hall and the way to the exam rooms."

"That all right. We will figure it out." Banji gave Maria a peck on the cheek, quickly moving away with a wink before she swatted his arm.

Akia, no intel on the layout of this place.

We don't even know if we have to go up or down—no windows in these cells. This is the desert; they often build underground to keep out the heat.

Hey! There is a window in this cell. So we are most likely above ground.

Look out it and get an idea of our location.

Banji looked at the window. Despite his Vukasin height, the window had been positioned so that it would be difficult for even a Vukasin to see out of it. If his brother had been here he would have had him to hoist him up, but only Maria was here and there was no way she could support his weight; she was just too dainty. But he could lift her up easily.

"Up we go, beautiful." Banji picked up Maria like she was a child and set her on his shoulders. She gave a startled squeak and started to protest until Banji asked, "Tell me what you can see out that window."

Maria wobbled a bit as she found her balance. Even sitting on Banji's shoulders, the window was still above her head. Maria used the wall to steady herself as she placed a foot on his shoulders to stand up. Maria had never been fond of heights, and her unsteady perch made her a bit dizzy. She forced her heart to slow down and concentrated on the task at hand.

Thick glass covered the window. Maria was surprised to see quite a bit of activity in the yard below. She never knew just how close she was to the outside world. The glass and stone walls blocked any sound.

"We seem to be on the second or maybe third story. It's kind of hard to tell since I can't lean out. The building seems to be built on a hill...no it's a canyon wall. We're in a canyon! I can see a lot of people on the ground. Looks like some sort of fight or training session. There are a lot of those creatures you guys seem to morph into." Maria looked down at Banji and immediately regretted it. Banji's quick reflexes to help steady her legs were the only thing that saved her from a nasty fall. "Out of curiosity...do your women also sprout fur and fangs?"

"Focus, Maria...but, no, they do not. Only the males transform, and not every male is capable of it."

"Hmm." Maria turned back to the window. "Some of the creatures—"

"Phased...when transformed, it is called

'phased.'"

"Some of the 'phased,'" Maria emphasized the word just for Banji, "out there don't seem right."

"What do you mean?"

"I don't know how to explain it. They just seem unnatural. They look off, and their movement is weird." She gestured to Banji that she was ready to get down.

Banji squatted down so Maria could hop off. Dusting off her hands, she looked up at the tall man before her. "I think there is an exit directly below us. It looked like a lot of people were coming from that area into the open area."

He laid a hand on her cheek. "Good job, little one."

Maria shoved his hand away, "I'm not that little." Banji just grinned at her because she didn't even come up to his shoulder.

If you are done making kissy faces at the female, we need to move up our plans. Just overheard the guard say that Sta'ling is on his way.

Banji frowned. Turning from Maria, he pulled a thread on the seam of his pants. Maria watched as he extracted a small device from the cleverly concealed pocket.

"What are you doing?"

"Making our friends watching us deaf and blind for a while."

With the touch of a few lighted areas, Banji sent out a pulse. With that pulse the lights flickered before failing. The women in the other cells started screaming.

"Save me from frexing idiot brothers! Banji, just how high did you adjust that thing?" Akia yelled from across the corridor.

"Hey I did my part; the monitoring devices are off, so quit your bitching and open these damn doors."

Banji chuckled as he heard his brother's voice in his head disparaging their parentage with curses about brothers. He wrapped an arm around Maria and pulled her close to his body. The only light they had was from the high window, and Banji knew that danger lurked in the shadows, so he wanted to make sure that he was close enough to shield Maria if necessary.

"We are all getting out of here, right?"

Banji sighed. "Maria, we talked about this already. Getting you to safety is our mission. But I promise we will return for the others."

Maria gripped Banji's shirt tightly. "You can't leave the other women here. They will be punished for our escape. Some of them may not survive."

For a brief moment Banji forgot his place and gently caressed Maria's cheek. "You are the only one who matters to me. I will see you safe."

Maria swallowed. She wanted to lean into the comfort of Banji's touch. Instead she stepped out of his touch and looked up into his eyes. He had beautiful eyes: a blue so dark that at a distance they looked almost black.

"I'm not leaving without them, Banji. It wouldn't be fair to trade my freedom with their suffering."

I think I'm going to need some help here, brother.

"I understand how you feel."

Maria slashed a hand through the air. "You have no way of knowing how I feel." Her voiced rose with anger and terror that had been long suppressed. "Those *bastardi* didn't rape and torture you. You didn't have to sit by helplessly as they abused and killed innocent women in front of your eyes." She raised an imperious hand when Banji tried to interrupt her. "If you do not attempt to save us all, then leave me here; maybe I could deflect some of the abuse from your escape. I've survived it longer and I am more likely to survive until you come back than they are."

"That's not an option," Banji growled. Why did Maria have to be so difficult? They were running out of time. He could hear his brother working the lock on their door. Down the hall he could hear the faint footsteps of approaching guards.

I'm coming in, Banji. Turn Maria towards the door so she doesn't see me coming.

She's not going to like the back-up plan, Akia.

If she is angry at us then that means she is alive.

Banji sighed and gripped Maria's shoulders. He turned her slightly while leaning down so he was face to face.

"We don't have time to argue, Maria. I can hear the guards on the way. If I try to take the rest of the women, we are almost certain to fail. I'm not risking you. I promised I would come back for those women; that is going to have to be good enough."

"Well, it's not go...od—" Maria turned midsentence when she felt a familiar prick in her arm. *Bastardi, all men are bastardi* was the last thought to drift through her mind before darkness consumed her.

Banji caught Maria has she collapsed into unconsciousness. He held her tenderly against his chest until his brother coughed and gestured to the door with his head. Right...they needed to get out of here.

CHAPTER TEN

Banji refused to let Akia carry Maria. His possessive need to have her in his own hands surprised him. In his entire life there hadn't been a single thing that he wasn't willing to share with his brother. That had even included the females they visited in the pleasure houses. For the first time in his life, he wanted something/someone for himself. He knew that it was unlikely, especially after the betrayal he saw on her face as she collapsed. He was doubtful that she would forgive him easily.

The sounds of grumbling guards grew closer. Banji hoisted Maria across his shoulders. He used a strip of the thin blanket to tie Maria securely to him. He wanted both hands free since they had confiscated his and Akia's guns. That left them with a couple of hidden knives and a garrote as weapons.

Banji and Akia moved out into the hallway. The wailing of the remaining women intensified. It was only through the acute hearing of a warrior and years of training to drown out distractions that Banji could hear the men just on the other side of the door at the far right. He drew two knives from hidden pockets on his belt.

Akia surveyed the hallway, his eyes lingering a moment on a set of sparkling eyes that watched him from the slit of one of the other cells. "I'll take point, brother. You concentrate on keeping our cargo safe while I clear us a path."

Akia and Banji didn't wait for the guards to make it to their cell block. Akia burst through the door, knocking one of the guards to the ground. He leapt and slashed a deadly dance. The first wave of half a dozen guards easily fell.

Akia turned at a shout from his brother. One of the injured guards had recovered enough to come at him, a dagger raised high in his uninjured arm. When he was almost to Akia, the man jerked and fell to the ground, his brother's blade neatly embedded in his neck.

Banji ran towards his brother, snatched the knife and winked. "I can't let you have all the fun, can I?"

Akia hollered, *"Remember that bar brawl at Tarek's pleasure palace where we saved one of the workers from a customer beating her?"*

"Yeah, she clung to your back like a noose vine when you stepped between her and her attacker.

I ended up having to guard your back because she wouldn't let go."

"Precious cargo—Maria is your noose vine. Let's cover our backs."

Back to back, the brothers stood. Their opponents surrounded them. The guards would feint and try to draw one brother away from the other, but no one wanted to get too close to the brothers. Two men had easily defeated a full squad of guards. While they knew their numbers trapped the men, each guard knew that if they were the first to attack, they would most likely die.

Banji and Akia inched their way towards the next set of doors. The guards moved with them, dancing around the edges of their blades. Banji thanked the gods that the guards relied more on size and brute strength to control prisoners in this area than weapons. He knew, however, that if they didn't escape soon, more men who were better armed would be coming. This crowd made a quick escape difficult. They were going to have to change from battlefield tactics if they were going to get out of there.

"Akia, break left while I break right. We have to make it to the ground floor if we have any hope of getting out of here."

The twins split in opposite directions. In perfect synchronization, the pair leapt up using the shoulders of the confused guards and the rough texture of the wall as stepping stones as easily as the best professional parkour course runner.

The lights flickered and then stayed on. Banji and Akia no longer had darkness as their ally. The pair needed to pick up the pace before they were trapped. They were just feet from a doorway with the symbol for 'stairs' on them. Next to the door, Banji spied the dirty food trays from the prisoners' last meals stacked neatly waiting for pick-up.

"Remember escaping from Instructor Mokti when we were seven?"

Banji grabbed a tray and ran through the doors to the stairwell.

"Just don't fall and break your arm this time!" Akia admonished.

He tightened the straps holding Maria to his back before he threw down the tray, planting a foot in the middle before pushing off with the other. He hadn't surfed down a set of stairs since he was a whelp, and it seemed more difficult than his memories of the act. He kept his center of gravity low to maintain his balance. Maria's dead weight complicated matters as she tried to shift each time he leaned a different direction.

Akia shook his head as he heard his brother's whoop of joy. Banji had always been the adrenaline junkie of the pair. Akia followed his brother down.

The straightaways were pretty easy to navigate, but the stairs made a one hundred eighty degree turn half way down. Akia and Banji crouched low, grabbing on the side of the tray to lift it just slightly. Sparks flew as they twisted their body weight to bring the meal trays up along the wall and across the door of the floor below where they had been held prisoner. One more story to go and they would be on the ground floor, they hoped. The centrifugal force didn't last long, causing the metal trays and their passengers to crash down on the second set of stairs. Great balance and physical training was the only thing that kept the brothers upright.

In a matter of seconds they had reached the next floor, which was blessedly the ground floor. They could hear the guards racing down the stairs, trying to catch up with them. If they could only get outside, they would have a better chance of escape.

Banji could feel Maria starting to stir. The dose of sedative that Akia had given her wasn't meant to last more than a few moments. It was designed to allow an operative to make a quiet getaway. Banji readjusted Maria's weight and used one hand to keep her soon-to-be-awake hands out of the way in case he had to defend them.

Akia and Banji ran down the corridor until they made it to the receiving area of the facility. A single guard stood watch near a door with a crystal

DNA lock. They would have only a matter of seconds to get out that door before the guards from the upper levels reached them. The guard by the door raised a stun rifle as he yelled into his communicator.

Whump! A pulse of energy pushed the escapees back. Maria fell lax once more. The twins staggered a bit but recovered quickly. The hours of Kavi stunning them over and over again to teach them how to overcome its effects proved worthy of their time and suffering.

Banji kicked the stun rifle from the frightened guard's hands. Akia grabbed one arm and wrenched it behind the man's back. The force placed on the joints allowed Akia to steer the man towards the DNA lock.

Akia slammed the man's hand onto the pad. The tell-tale snick of the lock releasing was heard just as the guards from upstairs spilled forth from the stairwell. Akia and Banji slammed the unlocked door open and dashed outside to what they hoped was freedom.

CHAPTER ELEVEN

What they stumbled into was far from the freedom they had hoped for. In front of them was close to twenty phased surrounded by a large crowd of guards. At first the crowd didn't seem to notice the twins and Maria. It appeared that the trio had stumbled into a training session, though it wasn't organized like the training the Tiaret were famous for.

Upon closer inspection, it seemed that this wasn't training but a gladiatorial battle. Numerous Vukasins watched the phased from raised balconies built across the canyon walls. They seemed to be cheering or jeering the men below. The guards simply acted as a corral.

Banji and Akia skirted around the crowd, hoping to escape in the chaos. The phased snarled and tore at each other with tooth and claw. Their actions felt rabid. Close up, Banji could understand why Maria said these creatures seemed unnatural. Parts of their bodies were disproportionate with the rest. They moved in jerky motions, as if they couldn't control their muscles properly. Almost all of them were covered in massive scars. While speech can be difficult when phased, it was possible, but all Banji heard from these creatures were snarls and growls. It was as if they had been reduced to nothing but wild animals.

They had almost made it to the other side of the crowd when a shout echoed through the canyon. Akia and Banji turned towards the noise and discovered Sta'ling Tanis overlooking the chaos below. He was far enough away from the brothers that his speech was distorted by the echo of the canyon and the roar of the crowd, but they could tell he had been alerted to their escape because his raised hand was pointing right at them.

The crowd suddenly falling into silence and turning as one unit would almost have been comical, like a dramatic scene from one of Banji's beloved Earth movies that Megan introduced him to, under different circumstances. Without the cacophony of the fighting, Banji could understand what the Butcher was saying.

"Guards! Seize them!" Sta'ling turned to the obviously wealthy spectators. "We will see how trained warriors stand against my pets. Gambling masters, give your odds!"

The guards nearest to the brothers charged after them. This lot seemed smarter than the guards for the prison cells because a few of them veered off to cut off the brothers' line of escape while the rest surrounded them.

They had been so close to freedom. Only a few more yards and they would have been able to grab a vehicle parked near the mouth of the canyon. Many of them were expensive models that Banji knew would fly like the wind. If they could break through the guards between them, they might still be able to make it.

Cover my back, Akia.

Always, brother.

Banji palmed both of his small knives, one in each hand. He allowed his body to partially phase, lending him strength and speed without alerting the enemy. It was a feat few warriors were capable of, and the technique was a closely guarded secret among the Tiaret.

He used his added speed and strength against the unphased guards. It seemed the guards had orders to take them alive, as most had only a stun stick in their hand. The stun stick had been designed for livestock, but even its use there was frowned upon. A touch gave an extremely painful jolt to its victim, and prolonged contact could knock them out. Banji's knives were much more deadly but required closer quarters to be effective.

Fortunately, Banji wasn't under any "no kill" orders. He faced the first jolt stoically. He had received worse at the hands of Kavi's trainers. The guard paled when the stun stick had no effect on Banji. One knife sliced the surprised guards throat, while Banji's other hand cut the wrist of a second guard nearby. Banji dropped and swept the legs out from under the injured guard. He plunged a blade into the man's neck, pulling it free with a spray of warm blood. Two down, four more to go before the path to the vehicles was clear.

Maria started to stir once more, and Banji knew that time was running out. The four remaining guards in front of him attacked him all at once. Banji ducked and twisted, evading their hands. He blocked most blows and traded them with punches and kicks of his own. He was trying to save his blades, and there were too many coming at him to make the garrote of much use. He was holding his own until one of the guards got the smart idea to grab Maria from Banji's back.

*****

Maria woke to a massive headache and being jostled around. It took her a moment to realize that Banji had her slung across his back like a sack of potatoes. On the heels of that realization was the fact that he was in the midst of battling guards. While her first instinct was to tear into Banji for going against her wishes, Maria was smart enough not to distract him in a life or death struggle. If they survived this she could rip him a new asshole then.

Strange hands ripped her from Banji's shoulder and were none too gentle about it. The cloth that Banji had used to tie her to him hadn't wanted to give way. Maria cried out in pain as their attacker pulled her until the cloth ripped. She was fairly certain that her ribs were bruised if not cracked because of it.

Maria's cry of pain sent Banji into a killing rage. No longer were his fists good enough. They hurt Maria—they would pay. Banji stabbed the guard in front of him and ripped his blade across the doomed man's midsection, disemboweling him. As the man tried in vain to keep his guts inside his body, Banji turned on the guard who held Maria.

Something dark must have shown on Banji's face because Maria paled and her eyes went wide and frightened, where before she only looked angry and in pain. Banji let out a battle cry and ran straight at the guard holding Maria. The guard obviously saw his death coming because he shoved Maria towards Banji and stuttered an apology before turning to try and escape the crazy man chasing him.

Banji leapt over Maria, knocking the guard

face first into the ground. All of his rage and fear for Maria spilled over. He slashed and stabbed at the man pinned beneath him even after he quit moving. He didn't stop until a delicate hand was placed on his shoulder. He whipped around to face a new foe only to stop cold at the frightened eyes of Maria.

"Enough, Banji...that's enough."

Maria was trembling in fear, but she held her injured ribs as she knelt next to Banji and tried to calm his killing rage. He had never seen a more courageous woman. After seeing the violence in him she shouldn't want to be anywhere near him, yet she still sought to soothe him. The bloodlust left him and Banji realized that there was still one more guard nearby. That didn't include any his brother was having to deal with behind them. Banji needed to know how many more enemies remained.

Akia....

Banji was hit with excruciating pain that he knew was not his own. Something had happened to his twin. He berated himself for not keeping an eye on his brother. They had promised their father that they would always watch out for each other.

Banji scanned the area. About ten yards to his left he found the last nearby guard and simply threw one of his knives. One second the guard was rushing them, the next the handle of a knife appeared in his eye. The man jerked mid-stride and toppled like a felled tree.

With the immediate threat handled, Banji frantically resumed his search for his brother. In all of their assignments they had never left the other behind. Either they both came home or neither of them would. It wasn't a pact that Banji was willing to break just yet.

Banji found a phased Akia on the ground being beaten by a half dozen of the deformed phased, while guards prodded them with stun sticks. At least three times that number lay dead around Akia. Why hadn't his brother called out to him?

Hold on, brother. I'm coming for you.

Gods save me from frexing idiot brothers. If I wanted your help I would have asked for it.

Banji took hope in the fact that his brother would still give him a hard time because he knew that Akia was in bad shape.

Banji, listen to me. You must leave me behind and get Maria to safety. She is the priority.

You can't ask that of me.

I'm not asking; I'm telling you to do it. The Khalon *needs to know about what is going on here. Those other women are coming from somewhere. These creatures are obviously some nefarious experiment. I am fairly certain that I recognized a prominent official from another clan in the spectators before all five hells broke loose—too many strange things all gathered in one place to be coincidence.*

So tell him yourself when we all get out of here.

Banji could feel the consciousness fading from his brother. It was only Akia's massive inner strength that kept him from fading into the darkness. Banji knew that his brother would be helpless if he passed out and stood up to run to his brother's rescue, like he had always before.

Banji, stop! I can't make it out of here without assistance and neither can Maria. You have to make a choice.

No....

Make a choice, Banji. Banji knew his brother was trying to manipulate him.

"No!" Banji's scream echoed off the canyon walls. He wished the guard under him wasn't dead because he needed an outlet for his rage. His brother or Maria…he couldn't save them both. The man who shared his entire past or the hope of his future?

Banji looked over at Maria's terror-filled, golden eyes and he knew then that there never really was a choice. He would do anything to save her, even sacrificing his beloved brother. He would live with the guilt of turning his back on his brother, but in the end Maria mattered more.

You are making the right choice, brother.

Banji closed his eyes and tried to hold back tears. He felt his brother's resolve to sacrifice himself in the hope that maybe one day Banji would find happiness.

Don't you dare, Akia. You live, gods damn it. I'm coming back for you. If you don't survive until then, I will follow you into the afterlife and kick your furry ass myself.

A pained laugh faded from Banji's mind as his brother lost his battle with consciousness. His body returned to his unphased form. Despite their victim's stillness, the deformed continued to bite and claw. They seemed to have forgotten Banji and Maria.

Sta'ling Tanis shouted once more. "Fools! Get the other two!"

Suddenly all eyes turned to Banji and Maria. So much for being forgotten.

"Time to go." Banji stood, pulling Maria to her feet.

"What about your brother?" Maria turned, looking for Akia, even as Banji propelled her towards the waiting vehicles.

"We're leaving him behind." Banji gritted his teeth, trying to suppress the emotions raging within him. "For now."

"You can't just leave him here!" Maria pulled against Banji's grip.

Banji tightened his hold to keep Maria from breaking away. He pulled her close to his face so she could see the pain and anger leaving his brother behind caused. "Don't belittle his sacrifice, Maria. He's trying to keep you safe."

Maria could see the resolve and the anguish in Banji's eyes. She started to lift her hand to his cheek to comfort him but pulled it back into a fist instead. What right did she have to comfort him? The brothers were honorable men. The last thing she should be doing is adding to Banji's guilt. So instead of arguing, she nodded and followed Banji as they made a mad dash to the group of parked vehicles. The pain in her side made keeping up difficult, but she didn't complain. Banji had enough to deal with, and telling him of her injury in that moment wouldn't change what they had to do.

As they ran, Maria called to Banji, "You know he's trying to keep you safe too."

CHAPTER TWELVE

Banji didn't respond as he shoved Maria into the nearest high-performance vehicle. He pulled the control panel so he could reroute the liquid crystal wiring. It had been ages since he had stolen a transport, but while performance may have improved the design, the controls were basically the same. The vehicle sprang to life with a throaty rumble, lifting about a foot off the ground. Banji was overjoyed to see that the fuel cells had a full charge.

Maria grabbed the side of her seat as the vehicle lifted from the ground. She had once seen a documentary about those people who live in the swamps of the United States; she wondered if this is what it felt like to ride in one of those air boats.

She bit the inside of her cheek to keep from crying out in pain. She felt the bone shift in her ribs. They were broken, not just cracked. He shifted the transport into reverse with a swipe of the ball hand control and whipped it around. It took a death grip on the seat to keep Maria from being thrown around. Her teeth ground together to keep the sound of agony inside.

In front of the vehicle were some of the guards that had caught up with them. The smart ones broke off to seek out vehicles of their own, though Banji doubted that they would dare to steal the transports of Sta'ling's wealthy guests like he had. Thankfully that had them rushing down the line to the Tanis service transports. The stupid ones stood in front of the transport with arms spread. Banji assumed that they thought they could block him in. Of course that only worked if Banji was unwilling to run them over. He wasn't. Just because he followed a code of honor didn't mean he was a nice guy.

The transport accelerated fast enough that the g-force plastered Maria to the seat. She tasted blood as her teeth cut into her cheek to keep from alerting Banji about how much pain she was actually in. Banji, on the other hand, seemed unaffected. He stood straight and tall in the driver's seat.

Maria watched the grim determination in his eyes and wasn't paying attention to where they were going. So she screamed as the first body hit the windshield. A quick succession of four more people slammed into the front of the vehicle. Banji didn't even flinch.

They were traveling at blurring speeds at the

base of the canyon, away from the compound carved into the rock that had been their prison. Banji's eyes never wavered from what lay ahead of them. Maria wanted to say something but kept quiet. She knew that if they were caught at this point that they would probably die. She had no desire to die just yet.

She could see the mouth of the canyon. Somehow she felt that if they could break free of these stone walls that would be the omen stating that they would make it. She felt hope for the first time in months.

Curiosity got the better of Maria and she turned in her seat to look behind them, wincing as the movement aggravated her injured ribs. She knew with her injuries she shouldn't move, but she wanted to see the hell hole that had been her home for months disappear in the distance.

She kind of wished she hadn't. The Tanis soldiers were too close for comfort. From the looks of the man crawling on top of one of the transports with what looked like some sort of missile launcher, their pursuers no longer cared if they were captured alive.

"Um…." Maria tapped Banji's shoulder. When he turned his attention towards her she pointed behind them.

Banji looked over his shoulder. "Dragon spider shit!" His hand slipped on the ball control and the vehicle veered dangerously close to the canyon wall. Maria screamed out a litany of Italian curses and started slapping at Banji's shoulder before he was able to get the transport back on course again. She leaned back in the seat, gasping for breath both because her ribs were throbbing from her outburst and because she had to calm her rapid heartbeat.

Banji grinned and shook his head at Maria's outburst. He had no idea what she had said, but he doubted any of it was flattering. Even with a translation device, she kept a part of her heritage in her language. Very few people had a strong enough mind to do that once the implant was integrated into their cerebral system.

Banji hit a couple of controls until a small hologram appeared in the corner of the windshield which showed what was happening to their rear. Three vehicles followed them. They weren't the fancy, high-performance sort that Banji had stolen. These transports were more utilitarian, most likely made for military use. Military vehicles tended to be slow and bulky; that might work in their favor.

"What is that?" Maria pointed to the large gun looking thing they were mounting on the roof of the lead transport following them. She had seen them hoisting it up when she had originally gotten Banji's attention. She knew what she thought it was, but she was hoping Banji would tell her something different.

They were on an alien planet after all and one could hope, right?

"A bit of ancient technology that was outlawed generations ago because it was considered too barbaric; your people would call it a cannon."

"*Madre di dios!* We'll be blown to tiny bits."

Maria screamed, covered her ears and shut her eyes as the first volley was fired behind them. It was childish but she somehow felt if she could make herself small enough that they would miss. She started saying her rosary prayers to try and keep herself calm.

Banji veered to the left, the transport turning up on its side as its chassis pushed away from the rock of the canyon wall. Sand, dirt and rock exploded from the crater that appeared where the transport had been just seconds ago.

Banji zigzagged back and forth as much as the tight space of the canyon would let him. The enemy fired on them three more times. Each time, Banji narrowly escaped the incoming ordinance. The last shot would have killed them if the idiots behind them hadn't overshot them. The shrapnel from the impact started a spider web of cracks across the crystal glass. The rear feed pixelated and blinked as the cracks spread until it went off entirely. They were now driving blind as far as the enemy was concerned.

Banji blinked away the sudden brightness of the day as their transport finally passed from the shadow of the canyon. It was much later than he had assumed; the sun was low in the vast desert sky.

"*Gratz Dio.* We are going to be okay. I asked god to just get us out of the canyon because if we made it that far we could make it to freedom." Maria visibly sagged with relief. They had cleared the canyon; that was her sign from god that they would be all right. But while Maria might look to omens for hope, Banji knew they still had a long way to go and he didn't have Maria's faith that the worst was over.

They were clear of the confining stone walls, but as Banji looked around he couldn't see any cover in the vast expanse of desert sand surrounding them. They needed help and he had to evade the enemy until it got to them. He pushed the transport to its max speed, hoping to outrun the enemy.

"Maria, just below my right shoulder on my shirt is a small pocket." Banji swerved, knocking Maria against the side of the transport as sand rained down on them from another explosive round. She couldn't keep the cry of pain quiet. Banji turned and narrowed his eyes at Maria but chose not to waste time arguing about keeping her injury from him.

"In that pocket is a transparent disk; it is as thin as your earth paper." Banji swerved again, throwing Maria against his side. A hiss escaped between her clenched teeth. He winced in sympathy, but being in pain was better than being dead. "Pull it out."

Maria gingerly did as he asked. It was so thin that if Banji hadn't told her it was there she would have missed it. The disk was about the size of Maria's palm, so it would have been easily hidden in a Vukasin warrior's hand.

Before Maria could ask what to do next, Banji hurled a wad of spit that landed in the middle of the disk. On contact the disk started to faintly glow blue.

"Eww...."

"Sorry, DNA is required to activate it. And not just skin or hair, only a bodily fluid works." Banji spared a quick glance behind at the enemy chasing them. They seemed to have run out of ammunition since they hadn't fired on them in a bit. But they hadn't given up the pursuit and seemed to be slowly gaining on them.

When the entire disk glowed, Banji told Maria to hold it up near his face. "Banji...alpha...zero...zero...two."

A mechanical voice sounded from the disk. "Voice code accepted. State channel."

"Buzzard raptor...one...one...one."

"Authorization required."

Banji cursed under his breath.

"Restate authorization."

"Emergency override: *Jinaria*...red...earth."

The disk crackled in Maria's hand. She almost dropped it when a loud angry voice bellowed through the device.

"Banji! This better be important. I was meeting with the Dyami council member."

"Kavi, geo-locate the emergency communicator and give us a safe haven. We've got bogeys coming in hot and heavy with no cover."

"I've got to quit letting you watch those Earth movies. I'm assuming that a 'bogey' is an enemy." Maria and Banji could hear Kavi moving around on the other end of the line. "This would go faster if you could give me an idea of where you are."

"Somewhere in the middle of the Tanis desert."

"Very funny. A more precise location if you please."

"If I knew where the frex I was I wouldn't be contacting you, Kavi. All I can tell you is that we escaped from a canyon and are now in open desert with the bad guys chasing us."

"Humph," Kavi grumbled on the other end. "It will take a minute for the array to find you."

"Please hurry," Maria pleaded.

"Ah good, you found the female."

"This female has a name." Maria went from scared to angry in seconds. Banji almost laughed as Kavi was caught off guard. He really liked that flash of fire that Maria would display.

Kavi coughed, "Yes...of course." An alert sounded from the communication disk. "Good, looks like we have a lock on your position."

"How far are we from a safe area? At the speed we are running I have maybe two hours of travel time before the fuel cells run out, but I estimate that our enemies will catch up to us in less than half that time."

"Good news is you are near the border. We've got a contingency of troops approximately an hour away due east of your position according to your tracker."

"By the moons! That change in direction will have the enemy gaining on us even sooner." Banji slammed a fist onto the transport's console. "This is just frexing great."

Maria asked, "Is there anything that you can do to help us before that?"

The communication disk went silent for a minute as Kavi considered options. "I'll give Reijo the information that you are coming in with the enemy on your backside. It is Tiaret warriors stationed there; I'm sure he will mobilize them to meet you halfway. But there is a chance that as *kijani-a* he may deem it too risky to enter enemy territory."

"If he doesn't we are lost, Kavi, and I have some information that you need to hear."

"I'll talk to Megan as well; if anyone can convince Reijo to get those soldiers to you as quick as possible it's her, Banji. I've got to go and get the orders out. Stay safe and come home."

The disk returned to its transparent color. Maria just stared at it.

"You may as well throw that out; it is a one-time use emergency communication device."

"Oh…I thought it was like a cell phone." She dropped the disk onto the floor of the transport. "So what do we do now?"

"Now we pray."

CHAPTER THIRTEEN

The sun was beginning to set and the two moons were high in the sky. Maria didn't find the same comfort in the unfamiliar night sky that she had back on Earth. Banji claimed they were nearing the coordinates Kavi had given them, but with the exception of the vehicles chasing them, she had seen nothing but sand and the occasional boulder.

At least they were down to only two vehicles on their tail. A little while ago, the fastest vehicle had caught up with them and tried to disable them by ramming their transport. Banji had done some fancy maneuvering and somehow forced the other vehicle up a rock out cropping, which acted like a ramp, launching the transport into the air. The top-heavy military transport flipped and landed. Maria wasn't certain anyone could have survived a crash like that.

The remaining vehicles kept pace but either couldn't catch up or were deliberately staying back.

Banji speculated that they were hoping to outlast them and would pounce if the fuel cells ran out.

Maria didn't much care at this point; her injuries over the months of confinement were finally catching up to her. Her side felt like an ice pick had been shoved there, and she was finding it harder and harder to breathe. The nurse in her knew her broken ribs had most likely shifted during their wild getaway and had probably punctured a lung.

There was no point in telling Banji. He couldn't do anything to help her; she would most likely need surgery. Distracting him as he tried to keep the enemy off of them would be counterproductive. She knew the survival rates for most major traumas on Earth; a single punctured lung was survivable with medical care. If it collapsed entirely she hoped they would have medical personnel nearby.

Maria laid her head back against the seat. She was so tired. She just wanted to rest her head against the door and sleep. If she could have, she would have laughed. How many times had she groused at Gio because he would fall asleep in the car while she was driving? Times had been much simpler then, when her biggest complaint was not having a conversation partner on road trips. Oh what she wouldn't give to be able to go back to those blissfully ignorant days.

She turned her head and studied Banji. Well, that wasn't entirely true. Despite the horrors she had experienced, she wasn't naïve enough to think they couldn't happen on her home planet. There were good people here, just like back home. And it was kind of neat to see the universe from a different perspective. And then there was Banji. The man confused her. It had only been a day that they had been together, but she felt drawn to him in a way that was more intense than anything she had ever experienced, even with Gio.

Maria looked up at the twin moons. She hoped Banji's brother was still alive. As long as he was alive there was hope for a rescue. She hoped Banji kept his promise and freed those other women from their cells. It hurt her heart to think what those women had to endure. Human trafficking was wrong on any planet, even if the people weren't technically humans.

Her breathing was becoming more labored; she couldn't get enough oxygen into her system. As much as she willed herself to stay conscious, she couldn't stop the darkness creeping along her vision. Pretty soon her body would succumb to natural processes.

Darkness descended and Maria's last thought was, "I wonder if I will wake up?"

*****

The hum of the hover engine was the only sound as the day fully gave way to night. Banji had been concentrating on staying ahead of their enemies, so he hadn't noticed the quiet until now. It was unnatural. While Maria had tried to stoically hide her pain, Banji had known she was hurting. She would let out an involuntary groan or hiss whenever he shifted directions. But he just turned towards dust clouds in the distance and...silence.

Banji looked over at Maria and was horrified to see her so pale, with a blue tinge to her lips. Her shallow breathing was barely a wheeze of air. He was no medic, but he had seen enough battle to know that she needed medical attention sooner rather than later.

The thought of a world without Maria had Banji praying to the gods, something he hadn't done since his first battle kill, to let him get her to safety in time.

Beep...Beep...Beep

The low fuel cell warning beeped in his ear like a death toll drum. He had been pushing the transport to its max, which drained the fuel cell faster. He had hoped it would hold out until they made it safely to Tiaret battle camp.

He hoped that the disturbance he saw in the distance was his clan coming to the rescue, but without a way to communicate, he couldn't be certain. It seemed all they had left was hope. He was out of ideas.

Banji chanced a look behind; it was difficult to judge distances since the Tanis were running without lights. As best as he could guess, the enemy was about the same distance as the vehicles racing towards them from the opposite direction. Hypothetically, he should meet the new players first since he was driving towards them and away from the enemy.

Hypothetical theory was a moot point when their transport lurched as all of the power failed. They hit the desert floor with bone-jarring speed. Banji was kind of glad Maria wasn't conscious for that.

Banji took stock. There wasn't really anything in the transport that he could use to defend them with. He was down to a single throwing knife and his garrote. *Damn the five hells!* Everything depended on who got to him first. Even then they would only have a chance if the vehicles he was driving towards were friendly. Banji normally had pretty good luck when it came to missions, but everything that could go wrong had gone wrong with this one. Banji wasn't willing to bet Maria's life on luck.

He crawled out of the transport and engaged the locks, sealing Maria in. It wouldn't stop anyone intent on getting to her, but it might slow them down long enough to let Banji get to them and stop them. Banji crouched in the shadows the bright twin moons cast and waited.

*****

He didn't have to wait long before the first vehicle full on Tanis soldiers arrived. They spilled out with stun sticks and pulse blasters in hand. Banji counted five men. He had to assume that the second vehicle carried just as many. His eyes flicked to the distance and back. He estimated he had only a couple of minutes at best before the Tanis reinforcements arrived.

Banji slipped around the transport, staying low to the ground and in the blackest shadows of the bright night. He was lucky that the moons were only partially full, so the shadows around the vehicle were deeper.

"We've got the traitor to his race cornered. Get out there and find him," the largest soldier barked at the rest of the men.

Banji lifted his lip in disgust. The soldiers milled about without order, only half-heartedly looking. If they had been Tiaret, they would have already quartered the area searching for him. Since the only cover available was the transport itself, the area around it would have been thoroughly searched. Instead they joked that they needed to make sure to keep the woman alive along enough for them to have some fun. One of the Tanis finally wandered over to the transport to look in through the windows. Before he could alert his comrades to the fact that the missing woman was unconscious inside, Banji struck like the deadly serpent the desert was known for.

The garrote cut into the enemy's throat, severing his vocal cords. Banji tightened the wire to the point that he nearly decapitated his victim. Unfortunately, while the man wasn't able to call out, he had enough wits to kick the side of the transport. The metallic clang echoed through the night and drew the attention of the other soldiers.

One of them raised the pulse blaster and fired. Banji used the body of the soldier he just killed to absorb most of the impact the sound wave generated. On most of the blasters had settings; the pulse would incapacitate its victim by making them dizzy and disoriented or knocking them out completely. However at its highest setting, the blaster could become a deadly weapon, rupturing internal organs and causing brain bleeds. Banji had no way of gauging which setting the blaster was on since he used a dead man as a shield. He assumed it was deadly force because they had attacked with cannon fire earlier.

Banji dropped the body and rolled away before the blaster could recharge for another round.

The soldiers were idiots for using weapons designed for large crowds against one man. The lag time between shots gave him an advantage.

He was up and running on the shifting sands. He tackled the next Tanis soldier to the ground. This one carried a stun stick. Straddling the soldier and using his weight as leverage, Banji pushed the stun stick against his enemy's throat. The man was strong enough to keep Banji from strangling him outright, but he cut off enough so eventually he would pass out, then Banji would finish him.

The soldier's death was taking too long. Banji roared in anger as two of the remaining men broke the crystal glass of the transport window and reached in after Maria. He reared back his fist and punched the man on the ground. He smiled as he heard a satisfying crunch and the man went limp. If he was lucky the fracture to the face was fatal.

Banji ran towards the two men who dragged Maria across the broken window, heedless of the bloody cuts they were causing. Banji let his rage that Maria had yet another injury distract him. He had forgotten about the leader.

The burly man stepped out of Banji's periphery and clotheslined him. Banji rolled on the ground, coughing and wheezing, as the bulked-up soldier leaned over with a feral grin. The man had a stun stick strapped to his waist but ignored it in favor of his fists. This was a sadistic bastard that liked to inflict pain. Banji wondered if this was the guard known as Krac that Maria had spoken of earlier.

Who the soldier was really didn't matter as he rained down blows on Banji. The Tanis soldier didn't give Banji any time to recover between hits. It had Banji so punch drunk that it took him a moment to process the fact that his enemy had been ripped away from him. When it finally dawned on him that he wasn't under attack any longer, he watched through quickly swelling eyes as chaos erupted all around him.

Thank all the gods of the universe that the dust in the distance had been the Tiaret men coming for them. A full squad quickly dispatched the remaining soldiers as a Tiaret transport sped by in pursuit of the other vehicle that veered off when they spotted the reinforcements.

A couple of medics tried to prevent Banji from standing and he waved them off, franticly searching for Maria. He found her lying deathly still next to the two dead Tanis men who had hauled her out of the transport. Banji pushed anyone who got in his path aside to fall to his knees next to her.

"She needs immediate emergency treatment," Banji croaked through his bruised throat.

The medics placed an oxygen saturation device over Maria's face. The lead medic barked a few orders and they rushed off to the nearest transport and were gone before Banji could make his way to the transport himself. He wanted to cry to the heavens that they left him behind, but he knew treatment for Maria was the priority, not his possessiveness of her.

He vowed that he would be there when she woke up, which meant he had to get through the debriefing as quickly as possible. Banji found the *kijani* of this unit, thankful that it was Allo, a trusted friend of both Reijo and the brothers.

"We haven't found Akia yet. Hopefully he will be in the last transport that escaped." Allo reached out to grasp Banji's forearm in a warrior's greeting.

"Akia isn't in that transport. We had to leave him behind."

Allo couldn't conceal his shock. He had never known either brother to leave the other behind.

"That isn't possible…."

"It's a long tale, Allo, but one that you and Reijo need to hear." Banji turned towards a transport, forcing Allo to follow. On his way, he kicked over the body of the soldier that nearly killed him; there on his wrist was the same tattoo he and Akia had seen on the abnormally strong soldiers they had battled. "Inform *Kijani-a* Reijo that this is a top-priority transmission. He'll know what to do from there."

Without thinking twice, Allo saluted and bowed, thus acknowledging that orders were received from a superior officer.

CHAPTER FOURTEEN

Banji knew that Ghaleb and Reijo were upset with what he had outlined to them. There were still way too many questions to be answered. Ghaleb wanted to continue discussing things but Banji didn't have the patience for dealing with royalty at the moment.

"With all due respect, *Khalon,* I've repeated my observations to you...twice. You have been debriefed. If you want more information, then I suggest you send someone to talk to Maria, if she survives."

"What do you mean 'if she survives'?" Ghaleb demanded.

"She was severely injured. By the time we made contact with the troops here, she was unresponsive and having difficulty breathing." Banji ground his teeth, trying to keep from yelling at the ruler of their planet. "I have not had the opportunity to see how she fairs because my *Khalon* and *Kijani-a* have kept me going over the same intel again and again."

The image of Reijo and Ghaleb flickered as Reijo exchanged a look with Ghaleb.

"I will be in camp by tomorrow afternoon. Megan wants to personally pick Maria up. We will discuss this further then. Go see to your lady." Reijo cut off Ghaleb's sputtered objection with a shake of his head.

Banji didn't waste a minute. He shut off the transmission and ran from the command center to medical.

*****

"Why did you let him go, Reijo?" Ghaleb demanded. "There were a lot of questions we still need answered."

"And you weren't going to get them tonight, Ghaleb."

Reijo went across Ghaleb's study to the small bar cabinet. He poured both of them a glass of what Megan called 'bourbon' even though it was green instead of the golden amber that the Earth woman was used to. He handed one glass to Ghaleb and then sat in a chair across from the desk. He took a sip, allowing the liquid to spread warmth throughout his body.

Reijo propped his ankle across his knee. He swirled the emerald liquid and watched Ghaleb intently.

"What?"

Reijo sighed, "For such a brilliant man, you really are an idiot, Ghaleb."

Ghaleb stopped mid-sip and blinked at Reijo, "I have no idea what you mean."

"He means you don't pay attention to the emotions of others." Megan walked into the study. She leaned down and kissed Reijo, then perched on the arm of his chair.

"How can you possibly know that? You weren't here for the rest of the conversation." Ghaleb frowned. "You listened in through your connection with Reijo didn't you?"

Megan quietly laughed. "Ghaleb, I've been here long enough to have a pretty good understanding of those I consider my friends. There is really only one thing that you are an idiot about, so it doesn't take telepathy to figure it out." She turned to Reijo. "So who was Ghaleb being an idiot about this time."

"Banji."

"Did they find her?"

"Yes, though she is in bad shape according to Banji." Reijo reached over and squeezed Megan's knee. "I am already making arrangements for us to go to her tomorrow. I told Banji you wanted to bring Maria back personally."

"You know me so well, my love." Megan tilted her had to one side and smiled. "So Banji, huh?"

Reijo nodded, "He seemed to care for her greatly. If I hadn't made Ghaleb let him go, I think he would have committed treason to get to her. He was quite angry at Ghaleb for wasting his time."

"I'm trying to save an empire here." Ghaleb frowned. "Besides, he was the one who wanted me included in this debriefing. I just wanted some things clarified."

"Oh, Ghaleb, you mustn't run off the men whose loyalty is without question." Megan shook her head at the monarch, "We need every bit of support."

"I wouldn't go quite that far, *jinaria*. If Banji is a true Tiaret, his loyalty has already shifted from Ivailo just like mine has."

CHAPTER FIFTEEN

Maria could hear unfamiliar voices around her. She wanted to open her eyes, but they felt so heavy. She was warm and numb; that was much better than the pain. Maybe she was dead and this was heaven. Something was on her face and it tickled. Why would heaven have bugs? She tried to bat it away but her movements were clumsy.

"Shhh…you need the oxygen infuser for a little while longer."

She knew that voice…and those hands. Her mind was too foggy to remember why she knew them, but they made her feel safe. Safe was good. Maria drifted back into the darkness.

"Should I be worried that she doesn't wake for long, medic?" Banji still held Maria's hand, his thumb gently tracing circles on her palm. A part of him was afraid that if he let go she would disappear. It killed him a little inside to see the monitors hooked up to her in this white sterile room. Beautiful women should be safe in cozy, warm rooms and smile at you when you come home to them.

Despite the cold feeling of the room, Banji had to admit that the modern Vukasin field hospital was a technological marvel. Everything was mobile and could be shifted around to accommodate almost any need. In the few cases that were beyond their equipment, a mobile slip stream platform was available that had enough range to send the patient to the nearest city.

Maria's injuries were fairly typical of battle, so they had been able to operate on her here. Cracked and broken bones, bruised organs, cuts, evidence of other medical procedures and sexual assault had also been found. It was a miracle Maria survived for months in that hell hole. No wonder she was so adamant about getting those other women free.

The injury that had nearly killed Maria was a punctured lung, which had collapsed before they got her back to the field hospital. While Banji knew in his head that the medics considered that a routine battlefield injury, it had still shaved years off of Banji's life until he knew she was safely out of surgery. The wounds were all closed, with only angry red scars remaining. Banji knew from experience that those would fade in a day or two. They had the ability to stimulate cell regeneration, so tissue healed in a matter of hours or days instead of weeks or months. But even though his mind logically knew she would heal at a rapid rate, it didn't do anything for the heart that ached seeing her hurt in the first place.

"She sustained prolonged trauma. Besides the punctured lung and broken ribs, we had to heal a number of poorly set broken bones; just about every organ had blunt force trauma." The medic lowered his voice and sighed, "Not including the trauma to her…." The medic couldn't go on and just looked at Maria sadly before snapping back into his professional mode. "Plus, she was malnourished and exhausted. It is only by the gods that she survived at their hands." The medic leaned over to check the readings on Maria's bedside monitor. "We have healed the tissue, but her body needs rest. It is doing exactly what it needs to."

Banji just nodded as the medic walked away. He tried once more to reach his brother along their shared telepathic path, even as he watched Maria sleep. Once again he was met with a cold void. Either his brother was too far away for them to make a connection or…he wouldn't think about the or at that moment. It was an unacceptable option.

He brought Maria's hand to his lips and brushed a feather-light kiss across her knuckles. "You've got to wake up, beautiful. Seeing you whole again is the only thing that will make this messed up mission worth it."

*****

Maria woke to a bright light shining through her eyelids. She was on a soft bed, under warm covers. For a moment she almost thought she was waking up in her flat back in Pisa. But raised voices soon debased her of that notion and all of the recent events came rushing back at her.

She took mental stock of her condition. She had obviously received medical treatment, as she was able to take a deep breath without gasping. She stretched and moved, amazed by the fact that she didn't have a single twinge of pain. She was a little stiff, which told her she had been lying there for a while, but other than that she felt better than she had in months.

Maria cracked her eyes. The light hurt, but she forced herself to open her lids so her eyes could adjust.

"I won't let you take her. I promised her that I would protect her. How can I do that if you take her from me?" Maria recognized Banji's voice, though she couldn't remember it sounding that desperate before, even when he raged at having to leave Akia behind.

"She would be safer in the capitol and you know it." The woman's voice sounded familiar. She must be one of the other women from Earth then.

Banji snorted. "You forget she was taken from the capitol before." He slashed his hand through the air and Maria smiled at the imperious gesture. "No. I will not trust her safety to anyone else."

"Reijo, do something with your soldier." The woman threw her hands up in the air and flopped down into a nearby chair.

"Banji, it would be best for Maria to be away from the battle and I need you here. Ghaleb is sending a larger force to aide you that will be here within a few days. They need leadership I can trust."

Banji looked as if he was about to waver but then straightened with resolve. "I stay with Maria. If she goes to the capitol, then so do I."

The two men looked as if they were about to come to blows.

"You know she is right here, and she is quite capable of deciding where she is going to go." Maria pushed herself into a sitting position as all three people turned with shocked expressions.

CHAPTER SIXTEEN

"No. I'm staying right here. I don't care if it is dangerous." Maria stared mutinously at Reijo. The *kijania-a* cursed Earth women as Banji stood off to the side with a smug look on his face.

"Maria, be reasonable…. You aren't a warrior like Megan," Reijo pleaded.

"You're right, I'm not. I'm a nurse, a healer…whatever you want to call it on this planet and I am needed here. Banji promised me that he would gather men to save the women we left behind. Those women are going to need someone who understands what they have been through. That person is me."

Megan's eyes snapped to Maria's and then narrowed at her husband, "What women is she talking about, Reijo?"

"*Jinaria*…."

"Don't you try to sweet talk me, you big

ape." She crossed her arms and glared at Reijo, "Ghaleb told you not to tell me didn't he?" She didn't give him a chance to answer before turning accusing eyes to Banji. "Did you know about this?"

"I was the one who reported the presence of the women to the *Khalon*."

"And you didn't think I should know about it?"

"I had assumed you would be informed, M'lady, considering your station."

"Station?" Maria turned to Megan, "I think I missed something. Does something special happen when you marry one of these guys?" She gestured with her thumb towards Banji.

"I forgot that you were kidnapped before the *Mate Avi Keiger*." Megan shrugged, "To make a long story short, I not only survived the trial that legally made me a warrior with all the rights that position holds in this society, but I also brought back an artifact that by their own ancient laws means I could take over the government if I want to."

Maria's eyes got as big as a dinner plates. "So you mean that you are the queen?"

"Yes and no. I could be if I wanted to, but as long as these guys play nice, I'd rather not." She gave a pointed look at Reijo. "Which means I need to know when something like this develops. Understood?"

"Yes, my beloved."

"Good. Now leave." Megan shooed the men out and turned back to Maria. "What about these women you were referring to?"

*****

It was almost three hours later by the time Maria had finished telling her story. She didn't go into detail about what they had done to her, but Maria could see in Megan's eyes that she understood some of it at least. It is a sad fact that too many women carry the scars of intimate violation.

"Those poor women. Do you know where they are coming from?"

Maria shook her head. "What little I could garner from overhearing the guards, their village was fairly primitive."

"Do you think they are from some remote area of Earth?"

"I can't say for certain. Without a translator I couldn't talk to any of them. But if I had to guess, I would say no."

Megan looked at her curiously, "Why? You said they kind of looked Polynesian and that they were petite like many Asian women. That doesn't sound too different from Earth and there are some remote communities in that area of the world."

"Well for one, their language didn't translate in my translator. Even if they couldn't understand me, I should have been able to understand them since this thing is programed with every known Earth and alien language the Vukasins know. But even if it was some obscure dialect that they didn't know about, they just didn't look human." Maria sighed and looked out the window of her hospital room, "It was something about the eyes. I've never seen eyes like that before. The color was amethyst, like polished jewels, and I have never seen human eyes shine the way that their eyes did. It was unearthly and beautiful." Maria turned her face back towards Megan. "At night, one of them would sing to calm the others I think. I have never heard a more haunting sound. You couldn't help but stop and listen. Even the *bastardi* guards would stop what they were doing to hear her."

"Then we will just have to go and rescue them, won't we."

*****

"No."

"But, Reijo…"

"Absolutely not, Megan."

Banji and Maria watched as the argument heated between Megan and Reijo. At first Maria tried to lend her voice to Megan's argument that the foreign women needed immediate rescue, but Reijo snapped at her that she wasn't a member of their military. Since then she had remained quiet, but

Banji knew from her body language that she wasn't cowed by Reijo; she was furious.

Reijo wasn't budging. He didn't feel they had the manpower to launch a rescue effort at this time and he wouldn't compromise the safety of the border towns the squadron was assigned to protect. In the end he was able to convince Megan that the rescue effort would just have to wait.

Banji saw the betrayal on Maria's face when Megan conceded. If he hadn't been watching her the entire time, he would have missed it because she locked it away behind a blank face before she let anger take its place.

They had met in the medic transport that had served as Maria's hospital room. Megan had insisted that Maria be included in the discussion because she had spent the most time as a Tanis prisoner. With her hopes crushed that they would help her free the other women, Maria started pulling the wires and tubes that monitored her off.

Banji, Reijo and Megan all tried to calm her down. She shoved each in turn out of the way, until she stood before them.

Yanking the last wire from her chest, she said, "So much for the *honor*," Maria sneered the word, "of the Tiaret. This is the second time a Tiaret has refused to help save those women." Hurt eyes cut Megan, "Though I had expected more from a fellow Earthling."

"You dare question my honor?!" Reijo, the man all of Vukas looked to for his iron control was turning red with rage. It seemed that Earth women had a talent for making men lose their control.

Any of Reijo's subordinates would be cowering in fear at this point. Five hells; even Banji flinched at the deadly threat in Reijo's voice. But Maria didn't cringe; she didn't cower. If possible, she stood taller, looking like royalty addressing someone beneath her with contempt.

"Yes, I dare." Banji watched in awe as the compassionate woman he knew her to be gave way to a fierce battle maiden. "You could find a way, if you really wanted to, but you have decided it is easier to leave those poor women to their fates."

"Even with Ghaleb's reinforcements, at best only a few could be sent. It would be suicide."

"Then give them the facts and give them a choice."

"You would send these men to their deaths so easily?"

Maria's eyes glistened and she swallowed. "Facing the possibility of death is never easy. I'm not naïve enough to think that none of your men may die, but I know that those women *will* die—or at the very least wish they had if they remain in Tanis hands."

Maria turned and headed to the door. She paused with her hand on the frame and looked over her head at Banji and Reijo. "There is a saying on my planet: 'All it takes for evil to flourish is that good people do nothing.' Well, I'm going to do something."

With that final statement, Maria stalked outside. She wasn't even sure where she was going and she wouldn't get far in her bare feet. She just knew that she had to get away from everyone else for a little while.

CHAPTER SEVENTEEN

"You better find me some men, Reijo. I'm going with her, with or without assistance. I made a promise to Maria and I intend to keep it. But I would much prefer to keep it with help. I'm not a fool after all." He looked out the door, searching for Maria. He found she had run almost all the way to the other side of the camp. He glanced over his shoulder at his commander and friend and saw Megan wrap her arms in comfort around her husband. With a single nod, Banji took off after Maria.

It didn't take long for Banji to catch up to Maria. She was walking instead of running at that point and was dashing away the tears that fell from her eyes.

"Maria, wait."

Maria didn't look back or stop. When she

was within reach, Banji took ahold of her elbow and turned her towards him. He pushed her unruly curls away from her golden eyes, taking a few tears with him. He wanted to wrap her in his arms until all of the hurt went away.

"Where are you going, Maria?" She refused to look at him and turned to walk away again. "What are you planning on doing?"

She continued to walk away. "Does it matter?"

He spun her around once more. "Of course it matters. You matter."

"I'm going to find some men to help free those women." Maria bit her lip and looked up at Banji. "And maybe find your brother."

"And where do you plan on finding these men? If these soldiers follow you against the orders of their commanding officers, they commit treason. That is a death penalty offense during a time of war."

"I know that, Banji," Maria huffed. "That's why I plan on heading into the town. I overheard some of the other soldiers talk about how there are a lot of mercenaries in the area. I figured I would get some of them to help me."

Banji closed his eyes and started counting. The woman was not just naïve, she was crazy. "And how do you plan to pay them? Mercenaries never take on a task unless there is profit in it." Banji crowded Maria, forcing her to back up to maintain any distance between them.

"I'm not an idiot. I will pay them." Maria's back pushed up against a storage container at the edge of camp.

"With what, *jinaria*?" Banji continued to invade her personal space until she could feel the heat of his skin.

Maria licked her lips and swallowed. Her mind short-circuited. He was too close. Part of her wanted him to get closer; she tried to ignore that part. Part of her wanted to shove him away, but she knew he wouldn't budge even if she tried.

"With what?" Maria parroted his words back to him, trying to give her mind a moment to process what it was going to say.

"Yes, you have to pay a mercenary, and right now you have nothing of value."

"That's not true," Maria whispered; but it was true. Hell, even the clothes she was wearing were borrowed from someone else. Everything had gone wrong and she was useless.... No, she wasn't. Maria's quick mind started clicking information into place. It was a skill that made her a damn good trauma nurse because she could anticipate what the doctor needed before he asked for it. What did she know? She had been kidnapped (twice) because she was female. She was offered as a reward for jobs done to men while in captivity. She had already been used as payment. She was valuable.

Banji knew he made a miscalculation when the fire flashed in Maria's golden eyes.

"That's not true. I have an extremely valuable commodity on this planet: Me." Maria pointed at her chest. "Me." Maria shoved past Banji and started pacing back and forth. The pain and fear of her experiences finally overflowed the dam in her mind that she had built. "I was stolen from my life because I was female. The Tanis took me because I was female. I was handed off as a reward because I was female." Maria turned with an angry glint in her eye and cocked her hip. She planted one hand there and gestured provocatively down her body with the other. "So, you see, I have all of the payment I need right here."

The idea of another man holding Maria, of her welcoming him into her arms and her body made something snap inside of Banji. She was his…HIS! Even if she didn't understand that yet.

Banji stalked toward Maria. "You would give yourself to the man that helps you?"

Maria's anger turned to trepidation as her golden eyes locked onto Banji's midnight ones. She had seen humor, anger, gentleness, even bloodlust burn in those eyes before, but it was an entirely different heat she was seeing in them now. She suddenly wasn't so sure that her plan was a sound one. Trading herself to someone to help free those women had seemed the logical course. At least she would have had a choice, where before it was taken from her. But now with Banji staring at her so intently, she wondered just what kind of dangerous Pandora's box she had opened.

"Answer me, Maria." Maria's back hit the storage container and Banji's arms came up and caged her in. "Would you give yourself to the man that helps you?"

"If it meant freeing those women from hell…." Maria's response started as a mere whisper, building in strength until she declared clearly, "Yes, I would."

Banji leaned down and feathered a kisses across Maria's cheek and down her throat. Maria swallowed as his warm breath heated the skin beneath his lips.

"You would let him touch you?" One hand caressed her side, pulling her body against him. Maria's hand instinctively went to Banji's shirt, fisting the material as if she never wanted to let him go. Maybe she didn't.

"Yes."

"You would let him taste you?" Banji licked and nipped along Maria's collarbone. She shivered.

Breathlessly, "Yes."

"Would you let him hold you, Maria?" Banji nipped the top of her right breast.

"Yes."

"Would you let him deep inside?" His nose nuzzled her as both hands slid down to wrap around her waist. "Would your slick heat welcome him?"

Maria could only gasp as Banji lifted her, wrapping her legs around his waist. If someone would have asked her before she left Earth if she liked forward, alpha men she would have said no. But something about Banji taking control felt right. It made her feel safe and like she wasn't alone anymore.

Maria buried her face in his shoulder. She was afraid that too much of her heart would shine in her eyes and she wasn't sure she had the strength to give him that just yet.

"Please Maria, my beautiful *jinaria*...tell me that if I help you that you will give yourself to me." Banji tugged on Maria's hair—not savagely, but just enough to force her to look him in the eyes. "Maria...."

Maia's eyes softened at the slightly pleading note in Banji's voice. Not even Gio had begged for her attention. The fact that this beautiful, strong man, who could have crooked his finger at any woman back on Earth and they would have tripped over themselves to come running, wanted her broke through the last of her resistance. After all, the only thing a woman wants is to feel treasured and desired, and there was no denying the desire blazing in Banji's eyes for her.

She felt powerful, something she hadn't felt since the first guard was allowed to rape her. This is what sex and intimacy was supposed to feel like.

She raised a hand to caress Banji's cheek and watched as uncertainty warred within his eyes with the passion she saw there. He was afraid that she would tell him no. She knew him well enough to know that even if it was difficult for him, he would walk away if she told him no. That fact just made her want to say yes even more. So she did.

"Yes, Banji." She kissed along his jaw and wrapped her arms around his neck. "Yes, I will give myself to you."

"Mine!"

CHAPTER EIGHTEEN

Banji carried Maria off through the camp. He finally had her in his arms and he wasn't letting go. Even when Maria, embarrassed by the whistles and playful jeers, tried to slide down his body to walk, Banji just tightened his hold, trapping her in his arms. He was taking no chances.

Thankfully, as a high ranking officer, Banji had been assigned his own private tent. As he entered the dim space, he lowered Maria to the ground but didn't let her go. He kept one arm wrapped around her. He loved the feel of her body next to his. With his other hand he gently cupped her cheek and brought her eyes to his. He wanted her so much, and not just to sate his lust. He wanted what he saw in Megan and Reijo...a lover, a partner, a future.

Banji stared into Maria's eyes for what seemed like forever. He didn't know everything she had been through, but he knew enough from the medical reports to know that he would never dishonor her by taking away her choices.

He laid his head against hers and sighed. "What are we doing here, Maria?"

Maria turned her head and kissed Banji, her tongue sliding over his lips, inviting him in. She caressed the front of his pants where an impressive bulge strained against the fabric.

"It feels like you know why we are here," Maria giggled against his lips. That sexual aggression was so out of character for her. Maria had always been the good pious Catholic. She had been waiting for marriage and never allowed her passions to rule her. But life changes, and after all the horrors she had experienced, she wanted to feel alive again. Banji's groan and desire-glazed eyes gave her that feeling.

Banji grabbed Maria and plundered her mouth with a kiss. He fisted one hand in her hair, angling her head so he could taste her throat.

"Please tell me you want this…that I am your choice, Maria." There was a vulnerability in Banji's voice that Maria had never heard before. It made Maria think that maybe there was a chance that this would be more than just tonight.

"You're my choice, Banji." Maria nipped at his collar bone. She tasted his skin as her hands and lips explored Banji's well-muscled chest. The men she had known back on Earth had never been this solid.

Maria nipped at his pec, soothing the small bite with a kiss. "I choose you."

Maria moved lower and lower, trailing kisses and declaring her choice. She found herself on her knees in front of him. She was unsure of herself, but she wanted to give this to Banji. She reached for the belt of his pants.

Banji reached down and caressed her cheek. "So beautiful."

Maria looked up at Banji through veiled lashes, and some of her uncertainty must have showed.

"As beautiful a sight as you kneeling before me is, you don't have to do this, *jinaria*." Banji's thumb traced the curve of her cheek. "I don't ever want you to do anything you don't want to do."

Maria bit her lip and looked away. Softly she said, "I want to...I'm just not sure how good it will be...I've...I've never...." Her voice trailed off and Banji realized that despite the things she had suffered, Maria was innocent in the ways of real intimacy.

Not that Banji was much better. While his experiences had been his choice, they revolved around paid services in the pleasure houses. This was the first time real emotion was involved in the act.

Banji turned her eyes to him once more. "In a way this is a first for me too. We'll discover each other together."

Maria opened Banji's pants and wrapped her hand around his cock. Her fingers didn't even touch. It was hard but soft at the same time, like steel covered in velvet. She could feel moisture pooling at the apex of her thighs at the thought of that warm hardness being buried deep inside her.

Before that happened, she wanted to show, not just tell, Banji that he was her choice...he had been her choice since they found themselves locked in a cell together. *Dio, was that only a few weeks ago?* It felt like a lifetime.

Maria steadied herself on Banji's thigh with one hand, while the other guided the glistening tip towards her lips. Tentatively her tongue darted out to taste the pearl drop. She smiled as Banji groaned. There was a power in this submissive position that she hadn't expected.

She looked up at him, surprised to find him watching her intently. Her gaze never left his as she licked him from base to tip before wrapping her lips around his member. She sucked him in while swirling her tongue around the head.

Banji's cock jumped and his knees nearly buckled. He recovered and remained upright, but

Maria's muffled giggle let him know that she noticed. That innocent outburst sent vibrations through Banji's entire body and he groaned loudly. He was ready to climax right there, but he wanted to be buried balls deep inside her when he did that.

Banji stepped away from Maria and pulled her from her knees.

Her eyes widened. "Did I do something wrong?"

Banji hated the uncertainty in her voice and kissed her until her eyes glazed with passion instead of tears.

"No, beautiful, you were doing everything right. So right that I wouldn't have lasted, and I have so many other things planned for you tonight."

He scooped her up and carried her as if she weighed nothing. He gently laid her on the small mattress of his field bed. Carefully he peeled away the borrowed tunic and leggings, like he was opening a precious gift.

Maria had to fight her instinct to cover up as Banji bared her to his sight. With each bit of skin revealed, his eyes darkened until they blazed with want. No man had ever looked at Maria like that, like she was a miracle and goddess all wrapped into one. It was a heady feeling. And she wanted more.

CHAPTER NINETEEN

Banji just stared at her beautiful naked form as he slowly stripped out of his own clothes. If he died tomorrow, he wanted to make sure that this night was imprinted on his brain and heart forever. When he had memorized the moment, Banji started at Maria's ankles and worked his way up.

He smiled against her skin, and she squirmed once his kisses reached her knees. His Maria was ticklish. He traced a finger up Maria's thigh and traveled over the dark curls that hid her from him.

Banji noticed how Maria's breath hitched, and she started to pant as his finger gently parted the curls and traced over the sensitive little nub.

"Please, Banji."

"Please what?"

"I need you."

Banji dipped a finger into her wet sheath. "Do you need me here?"

Maria's hips thrust against his hand,

"More...."

Banji gave her more. He inserted another finger as his tongue tasted her. Maria moaned and ran her fingers through his hair. She held him to her, silently demanding. Banji suckled her sensitive clit while his fingers worked inside of her. He knew he had hit the right combination when her body started to convulse around his fingers and her breathing came in short gasps. With a final flick of his tongue against her nub, Banji lifted his head to watch Maria fall apart.

Her orgasm hit hard, and she called out Banji's name. Masculine satisfaction smirked across his face while Maria stared at the ceiling in wonder. After he made sure of Maria's pleasure, Banji was ready to move on to their mutual pleasure.

"We aren't done yet."

Banji crawled up Maria's body, kissing and nipping a sensual trail until he was over her. Maria smiled and wrapped her arms around his neck. She arched her back to reach him, kissing him with every bit of passion and wonder he had just showed her.

Banji braced his arms on either side of Maria's head and moved his body to align with hers. As his shadow fell across her, Maria's face went from sensual wonder to terror. In a matter of seconds, she was pushing at Banji.

"No! Get off of me!"

Maria was having a panic attack. Banji quickly moved to the side and Maria turned away from him. The field bed wasn't very large, and Banji was grateful for that. He didn't want to be far from her, but she scooted to the very edge of the mattress.

"Shh...*jinaria*. You are safe here." He reached over and gently wiped the tears from Maria's face. She buried her sobs into the mattress. Banji wanted to hold her but was afraid that would hurt more than help, so he rubbed her back and made soothing sounds at her.

Eventually her shaking stopped, but she continued to cry.

"I'm so sorry, Banji."

"You have nothing to be sorry about, little one. If anyone should be sorry it is me. I shouldn't have pushed you so soon after...." He let the statement trail off, not wanting to go into detail of what happened to her.

Maria rolled over to face him. "Don't say that. I wanted this...still want it. I know you are not like those men, but for a moment it felt like I was back there in that room with the Doctor watching." Maria ducked her head. "I understand if you decide you don't want to be with me."

Banji reached for Maria, hugging her close. He didn't know what to say to make it better, so he said nothing. Maria squirmed and turned to face away from him. For a moment he worried that he had done the wrong thing pulling her to him, but she then pressed her body against his. She pulled at his hand, entwined her fingers with his and laid them both across her waist.

"I need you to hold me, but at the same time...right now, I need the breeze on my face so I don't panic. How messed up is that?"

Banji used his foot to toss a blanket up from the foot of the bed so he didn't have to let Maria go. It took a little maneuvering, but he eventually covered both of them without letting go of Maria's hand.

"Say something, please, Banji."

Banji sighed, "I wish I could fix it, Maria. If I could change what happened to you I would."

Part of Maria wanted to jump in and tell him that she knew he would and that that was one of the reasons she loved him. Loved him? *Madre di dios*, she did. Maria took a deep breath, trying to stop the tears from starting again.

Banji felt Maria try to hold back her tears. He was amazed by her. She was fighting to conquer the demons other men gave to her. She was one of the strongest people he knew, even if she didn't see it herself. He didn't want to give her up, but he cared for her enough that he would if it was the best thing for her.

"Do you want me here, Maria? If you are afraid, I can—"

Maria twisted towards him and pulled her hand free from his grasp. She took both hands and cupped his face, forcing him to look into her tear-streaked eyes.

"I don't just want you, Banji. I need you. I need you, but I don't know if I can be what you need. I'm a selfish bitch because I know you will stay just because I need you and that isn't fair."

"*Jinaria*, don't you know that before I was tossed in your cell I was only living a half-life? I went through the motions, but there was no meaning. It was follow orders and do what you are told. I didn't even really have to think. You gave me meaning. When I look at you, I have a reason for being here." Banji kissed the tears from Maria's eyes. "You don't even know how much of a gift you are to me. If this is all we have, it is enough."

Maria gave him a watery smile and Banji kissed her on her nose.

"But I have faith in you...in us. We will have it all. The wait will just make it sweeter."

CHAPTER TWENTY

Maria woke from a fitful sleep before the sun breached the horizon. She felt physically safe sleeping in Banji's arms, but her mind just wouldn't quiet. His words haunted her. He had faith that they would have it all. Did that mean he wanted forever with her? Or was he referring to just sex? She wanted to believe that he wanted more—needed to believe it. Her own feelings were scary in their intensity. Was this what real love and passion felt like? She didn't know. The love she had with Gio had developed over years. They had grown up together and it was just assumed that one day they would marry. She knew she loved Gio, but she was drawn to Banji in a way she never was with Gio. It was scary because they had only known each other for a few days and Maria questioned if real love could develop in such a short time. Yet they experienced more together in those few days than most couples would have to endure in a lifetime. So her mind argued itself in circles.

If she were honest, it wasn't just her feelings for Banji that confused her but the way he treated her as well. Yes, he was overbearing at times, especially when it came to her safety. But even with all of his strength and alpha-male tendencies, she knew she would always be a priority with him. She had heard the medics when they said Banji couldn't be pulled away from her when she had been unconscious. A person only does that to someone who matters to them. Last night had proved he cared even more. After her panic attack, he just held her and seemed content with that, even after Maria had promised to give herself to him. Gio would have sulked and whined because he hadn't gotten his way.

Gio and Banji were so different. Gio was like the popular boy in school while Banji was a man you could count on. Gio was her girlhood dream, but little girls grow up eventually. Maria was no longer the innocent girl. If she was going to have a man in her life, it needed to be someone she could count on even in the bad times. Banji seemed to be that kind of man.

Maria rolled toward Banji's sleeping face. She reached up and traced the stubble-covered chin with a finger. She was certain now that her feelings for Gio had been comfortable infatuation; but was she still ready to give up her old life for a new one here on Vukas? She missed her *Nonno*, but her grandfather had probably resigned himself to her being dead. It had been months after all. She knew without a doubt that even if Gio had waited for her, she couldn't be with him in that way anymore. Even her apartment was probably occupied by someone else by now. If she went back, she would have no job, no fiancé, no home. Here she had Banji and a purpose. Would it be enough?

Banji startled her out of her thoughts by grabbing the fingers that petted his skin. He lifted them to his lips and kissed them gently.

"You are thinking too much; I can tell. Have you discovered the great mysteries of life yet?"

Maria smiled, "Perhaps."

Banji rolled towards Maria and cupped her cheek before leaning in for a kiss. "You are so beautiful to wake up to in the morning."

Maria snorted a laugh, pulling at her mop of shorn hair. "I'm fairly certain I look like a cartoon character with my hair going every direction."

"I'm not sure what a cartoon is, but if it looks like you it must be adorable." He hugged her close, his massive erection pressing into her bare stomach; they hadn't redressed after last night's debacle.

Banji heard Maria gasp at the obvious evidence of his arousal. "Ignore him; he has a mind of his own, especially in the mornings."

Maria licked her lower lip, a move Banji recognized as something she did when she was gathering her courage. "What if I don't want to ignore him?"

"I won't lie, both heads are saying, 'glory to the gods.' But despite that initial kneejerk reaction, I don't want you to feel like you have to do anything. Whatever you are willing to give, it is enough."

"I know," Maria sighed. "I thought about what happened last night. It wasn't all bad."

"Some parts were very, very good." Banji waggled his eyebrows at Maria and she had to stifle a giggle.

"Yes, well…. As I was saying, I didn't panic when I was giving you a blowjob."

"Blowjob?" Maria pointed at Banji's erection and then at her mouth. "Ah, I see."

"That is a very submissive position. Yet, even in a position when you had the control, I wasn't afraid." Maria took a deep breath and rushed through the rest. "And when you had your mouth down there on me, I didn't panic. In fact I really wanted you to be inside me."

"But you did become afraid when I went to do just that."

Maria looked away from Banji, "I'm sorry." Banji hugged her close and Maria pushed him away so she could look into his eyes. "I want to try something, Banji. But I don't know if it will work."

Maria pushed herself up on her elbows so she could look down on Banji. He saw her resolve and her trepidation. She was the most beautifully brave person he had ever seen. She was facing her fears, not for death and destruction, like a soldier would, but for life and love. Banji wanted to see her smile.

"If it involves you with any part of your body on me, I am your willing experimental subject." Banji grinned at her lasciviously. He crossed his arm beneath his head and lay back, spread for easy access. "Do what you will, *jinaria.*"

"You call me that a lot...but it doesn't translate in the translator." Maria pushed herself up to her knees and crawled down Banji's body. "What does it mean?"

Banji gasped as Maria ran her fingernails up his thighs. "It means...beloved, my treasure, the one who is most dear to me...roughly anyway."

Maria braced her hand on Banji's thighs and leaned forward, bringing her face closer to his. She searched his eyes. "Is it true?"

Banji looked straight into Maria's eyes. He let her see the heat and longing captured within, but he also let her see the vulnerability. Vukasin men weren't supposed to want a woman. Even if they were lucky enough to be able to breed to continue their line, women weren't allowed to stay. At least that was the way things had been for generations. That all changed when the women from Earth arrived. Thanks to Megan and the Spear, now a woman could choose to stay with one man until death separated them, like the stories of old. Banji hadn't thought much about the changes to their world because he never really thought that they would affect him, but with Maria he found he wanted forever.

"More than anything…" Banji finally responded breathlessly.

*****

Maria crushed her lips to Banji's as she straddled her legs across his muscular hips. She was done worrying about what if. She wanted to live— really live in this moment. No past monsters or ghosts.

Maria broke away from the kiss and ran her hands across Banji's muscular chest. Never did she think she would have a man who looked like this. He was more than drool worthy and put even her best celebrity crushes to shame. But he was so much more than a beautiful man. He was passionate, honorable and could be so terribly gentle or incredibly fierce. And he looked at her like she was the greatest gift he had ever been given.

Her lips followed her hands. *So far so*

good...not a single twinge of panic.

Banji caressed Maria's unruly hair. He gently tucked a longer strand behind her ear. "What are you thinking of, Maria?"

"Can you stay like this? With me on top?"

"I can do anything you need me to." Banji waggled his brows at her, "Especially if it means I get to feel you wrapped around my rod."

Maria giggled and blushed like he had hoped she would.

Maria had no experience leading a sexual encounter. She rocked her hips experimentally. His shaft provided enough sensation to heighten Maria's arousal. It wasn't long before her natural response lubricated the friction between them.

Maria heard Banji groan as he raised his hips, increasing the pressure between them. She quickened her pace and lengthened the stroke of her hips. Banji's hands grabbed her hips and started to control the rhythm. Maria threw her head back and moaned. She was so close.

She circled her hips and stumbled upon an angle that had the head of his shaft sliding slightly into her sheath. It was unexpected, and her eyes snapped open and she looked down at Banji wide-eyed.

"The choice is yours, *jinaria*. It will always be yours."

Maria's eyes softened and she angled her hips to slide him deeper. He was large like most Vukasins. She undulated her hips, taking a little more each time until he was fully seated.

She lay forward on Banji's chest, giving herself time to adjust. He wrapped his arms around her and nibbled on her neck and ear. She was kind of surprised that hadn't caused even a twinge of panic. It seemed as if she had been right in that Banji looming over her last night was her panic attack's trigger. It wasn't the sex itself, because she was filled to the brim with Banji and her only thought at the moment was that she wanted more.

Maria nipped Banji's ear and suckled away the sting before pushing herself back up. She slowly found her pace, and she loved watching Banji's face change with need. He reached up to caress her breasts as they bounced in front of him but stopped just short of touching them.

"May I, please...."

Maria took his hand and placed it on her chest. His palm kneaded as his thumb caressed her nipple into a stiff peak. She shivered. When he sat up to suckle at her breast, the sensation traveled all the way to her core. Banji growled as her wet heat spasmed around him. It was such a sexy sound.

Maria rode him, the new angle rubbing delightfully both inside and out.

"Faster...oh, please...*dio*," Maria panted. Banji raised his hips in time with each of her down thrusts. His tongue and lips devoured her neck and breasts. She could feel the scrape of his teeth against her throat.

Banji bit her shoulder as her climax crashed over her. The slight sting of pain sent her over the edge of the precipice she had been standing on. Before her body even finished the last of her aftershocks, Banji was on his knees and flipped Maria over onto hers.

He was driving into her fast and hard, and she reveled in his loss of control. Being with Banji made her feel alive. Banji needing her so much he forgot to be gentle made her feel powerful and feminine. Maria closed her eyes and pushed her body back against Banji's frenzied thrusts.

Instinct was riding Banji hard. Everything in him screamed at him to claim Maria. Never had any female evoked such a response from him. Try as he might, Banji was lost when Maria arched her back and bared her neck to him. He couldn't stop the partial phase if he tried. He thrust into her a few more times and growled before his teeth struck at that spot where her neck and shoulder met.

The sharp pain caused Maria to cry out. But soon her cry turned into a moan as heat, lust and pleasure swamped her system. Who knew a love bite could be so erotic? That potent chemical cocktail had her riding the crest of a new climax. The suckling pull of Banji's mouth had her sex squeezing his manhood. All he had to do was reach around and flick her clit, and she crashed into climax once more.

Banji licked the small wound he had caused to speed its healing as Maria broke apart once again in his arms. This time he went over the edge with her, calling out her name. Together they fell into a satisfied heap without even disconnecting from each other.

Banji wrapped Maria in his arms, spooning her close to him. He really wished that they could stay like this forever, but the day awaited. Both he and Maria were needed by others. But he vowed that as soon as they rescued his brother and the other women, he was taking Maria away from everyone so they could spend a few weeks just the two of them together. He wondered what Maria would think of that?

CHAPTER TWENTY-ONE

"Are you sure you want to volunteer for this, Allo?" Banji rubbed his neck; things were more complicated by the minute. "You heard Reijo. This could very well be a suicide mission. Add that to the fact that you would be forfeiting your military career...."

Allo waved a hand at the three other men sitting behind him. "We know. I can only speak for myself, but I know this is the right thing to do. Soldiers talk, Banji; you know this. Every one of us heard about the injuries Maria had when the medics got a hold of her. No one, let alone a female, should have to endure that kind of abuse. Someone has got to take a stand."

"Besides, if we rescue them perhaps one of the women will look at us the way Megan and Maria look at you and the *kijani-a*," a young warrior barely out of the den piped up. Banji had to search his brain before he remembered that the youth was called

Boroff.

Banji glared at him. "Those women have suffered enough at the hands of Vukasins. I will not tolerate any man on this mission trying to pressure them into a mating."

Boroff lowered his head as a sign of submission. "I don't want to pressure them, but that doesn't mean that I don't hope for a female of my own one day."

The rest of the men grumbled their desire for a woman of their own as well.

Maria had entered the back of the tent and caught the last part of the men's conversation. Fewer men had volunteered than she had hoped, and it took weeks longer than she had expected, but she could understand their fear. There were different types of honorable people: those who found their honor in following the rules and laws of their society and those who found their honor in doing what they believed was right even if it wasn't popular. Most people, it didn't matter if they were on Earth or Vukas, were followers; they needed someone else to tell them what was right and proper. It took courage to swim upstream, so to speak.

Maria couldn't fault them men who volunteered to help them rescue the other women for desiring a relationship. Wanting to be loved and matter to someone was a basic human drive. She didn't see any reason why the Vukasin men would be any different. Every creature with the capacity to think for itself sought out love and companionship.

Banji was getting frustrated because he didn't want the men to think they were entitled to anything from the captives they rescued. Most people only saw Banji as the 'fun' twin. They didn't see how much empathy he held for others. They never paid attention to the fact that Banji made sure the little details were taken care of. But Maria noticed. Each time another facet of Banji's heart and soul was revealed, Maria's heart took a little more of Banji inside. Pretty soon Banji would replace her heart entirely.

"Did Reijo give us the translators we asked for?" Maria stepped into the middle of the small circle of men.

"Not as many as I would have liked, M'lady."

Maria turned to a distinguished-looking man. "Eligio, right?"

"Yes, M'lady."

"Weren't you part of the medical staff that treated me?"

"I was." Eligio gave Maria a wan smile. "My clan is responsible for this mess. The least I can do is attempt to help fix it."

"You're a Tanis?" Maria's mouth hung open

a bit.

Allo jumped to Eligio's defense. "He is a loyal member of the Vukasin military and a decorated officer."

Maria turned to Allo. "I meant no offense, sir. I was merely surprised." She turned back to Eligio. "It must be difficult at times to fight against those you once called family."

"I miss my cousin the most. She was one of the few women born in these last few generations." Eligio sighed. "Her father, as well as my own, cut off contact and forced her to do the same when I refused to be recalled to Tanis lands."

Maria sat next to Eligio and patted his thigh. "I understand. I miss my *nonno*, my mother's father. He was all of the family I had left. It is hard when you don't have contact with those you love. What's your cousin's name?"

"Ghita…she's the reason I stayed. She is just a child right now, but one day…" Eligio looked Maria in the eye, "One day she will be an adult. I want the world to be a place where she can have the choice to be happy when that happens."

Maria smiled at him and patted his thigh again, and the moment was over.

Eligio coughed. "Back to the matter at hand…. We were only given a half dozen translators."

"That is not nearly enough. There were more women than that shoved into a single cell. In the area I was held there were at least five cells filled to capacity and there was no telling how many other cells in different areas also housed women." Maria turned to Banji. "Could you talk Reijo into giving us a more?"

Banji sat down in the circle of men and pulled Maria into his lap. The protective part of him wanted to leave her here so she would be safe. He knew that Maria wouldn't allow that; besides, his possessive part wanted her where he could be there to protect her.

"He already gave us what he had on hand. We could wait for more to come from the capitol, but it would mean a delay in the mission."

"We can't wait, Banji." Maria shuddered with the memories of her captivity.

"I agree." Banji wrapped his arms around Maria until she relaxed into his embrace. "Plus, I am hoping to find Akia among the prisoners."

"Is there anything else we need to know?" Allo leaned forward. He was willing to risk his life to save these people, but he refused to go in blind.

"How much did Reijo brief you on my report?"

Allo shrugged. "We were told the Tanis had a prison nearby and that there may be off-world women being held there."

Banji absently drew circles in Maria's palm. "That is true, but there is a lot more that you need to know. For one, Sta'ling Tanis is there."

"Please tell me our orders are to kill that bastard." Maria and Banji turned to the final volunteer, who up until that moment had remained silent. It was a man Banji was unfamiliar with.

"You are?"

"Daya, ordinance expert." Daya didn't even look up at the people around him.

"I take it from your tone and question that you are familiar with The Butcher."

Daya dug a rock out of the compacted soil with the point if a very large blade. When the rock popped free, he spun the knife in his hand and sheathed it in his boot in a move so fast that it would have been missed if everyone hadn't been staring directly at him.

"My best friend was one of his 'test subjects.'"

Daya looked directly at Banji with unblinking eyes. It took every ounce of self-discipline not to look away from Daya first. Not even Reijo, the man Banji respected the most as a warrior, had made him want to show submission in such a fashion with a single look. Daya was the ultimate predator that Sta'ling had wanted to create.

Banji was certain that in a way Sta'ling had created him, even if it was indirectly.

"We don't have time for personal vendettas," Banji announced.

"However, should the opportunity arise. I doubt any here will mourn the man." Banji glared at Maria after she added her say. Maria just raised a brow in challenge. Banji sighed.

"The second thing you need to know is about the deformed." Banji ran a hand through his hair. He wasn't sure what to tell about the things he and his brother had battled. "It seemed that Sta'ling or someone else within that facility is experimenting again. I don't know how or why, but they have discovered a way to force men into a phased state. They are stronger and more animal than man."

Maria coughed to get the men's attention. "You need to know that most of the males that were experimented on were the vulnerable in your society...the poor, maybe even homeless. Banji told me once that not every man was able to phase."

Eligio looked back and forth between Maria and Banji. "A man who can phase should be able to at least be a common soldier. They wouldn't be considered poor."

"Then we can assume that the Butcher found a way to force the phase on someone without that ability naturally," Daya interjected. "The bastard just can't leave nature alone."

"That would definitely explain the unnatural feeling those creatures gave off in battle. They didn't even seem to be people any longer." Banji went on to explain the events of their battle of escape and what little they could give them about the compound.

"So is everyone on the same page?" Banji asked.

"Break into a fortress, save the damsels in distress, kill off an army of freaks," Allo summarized.

"Don't forget rescue Banji's brother," Maria added.

"Of course we won't forget Akia. I'm never going to let him live it down that I had to come haul his ass out of an enemy prison." Allo winked at Maria.

CHAPTER TWENTY-TWO

Maria looked out the window of their transport. The sun was high in the sky and they had been traveling since before dawn. She was having to concentrate really hard not to start whining like a petulant child on a road trip.

New information had come in during their meeting with the volunteers. The prison was evidently just a holding facility, but they were taking those kept there to another location. Reijo decided that an organized military raid would be best against the valley site. He talked to Banji and Maria and they agreed to try and discover where the Tanis were taking the women.

They were heading to a border town in disputed territory. All the warriors agreed that they needed more information before storming the castle so to speak. Maria had felt useless while the men planned their course of action. Logically she knew that this was their area of expertise, but she never had played the damsel in distress very well.

Maybe it was the heat getting to her, or maybe it was the bumpy ride in their transport, but Maria's mood was getting worse. Supposedly they would be near their destination when darkness fell. The men had decided it would be best to camp out in the desert and enter the town by daylight.

"What's Earth like?" Boroff leaned forward between the seats.

Maria scrunched up her face. "Um...I guess it is a lot like Vukas. We have different climates like deserts, mountains, coastal areas, jungles."

"Is it true that there are as many females as males?"

"I don't know exact numbers, but basically gender is split about fifty-fifty if you take the entire world population as a whole."

"And your females, they stay with one male?"

Maria chuckled a bit. "That is a lot more complicated. The majority of relationships are male and female pairings, but in some countries people are allowed to form whatever type of relationship that makes them happy. Two women, two men, sometimes three or more people together."

"That seems unnatural," Daya interjected.

"Some people on Earth would agree with you. But even here on Vukas males sometimes have intimate relationships with other males."

"That's only because there aren't enough women and they are weak."

Maria shook her head. "That is a narrow-minded excuse, Daya. Would a weak person open themselves to hate and ridicule? It takes a strong person to go against the masses to find your happiness."

"But they can't make children and then their line dies out."

"Love shouldn't be about whether or not you can make a child. I do understand your point of view. My religion holds similar ideals; they believe anything other than a man and a woman together is a sin."

"If your gods tell you it is wrong, then why do you play the advocate?"

"Religion is not my god. It is humanity's interpretation of various teachings. Man is fallible. It would be the height of narcissism to think that mere mortals could fathom the mind of god.

"I worked as a trauma nurse, a medic that specializes in injuries that could be fatal. I saw what hate and ignorance can create. I also saw people of immense emotional strength and character. But most of all I saw the power of love." Maria leaned her head against the window of the transport and stared at the endless Vukasin sky. The marveled at how similar it was to Earth's, but it was still different. "The love I saw knew no gender, no social norm…it just existed and was powerful. Something like that could only have been created by god, and I wasn't arrogant enough to think that I had any right to judge what god had created."

"Hmm…you are a very wise female, Maria Russo." Daya pulled a blade from the sheath on his forearm and began sharpening it.

The rest of the transport fell into a comfortable silence and Maria closed her eyes. She should try to rest while she could; there was no telling when she would get the chance to again.

*****

How do I keep her safe? By the moons, I wish Akia was here. He was always the planner, I was just the muscle. But muscle isn't good enough anymore. If something happened to Maria it would break me. I would make rivers of blood flow until death stopped me.

"Nothing will happen to me. I'll be careful, I promise." Maria blinked sleep from her eyes. She was kind of surprised to hear Banji voice some of his fears. He tended to hide his insecurities behind bravado. Maybe he was better friends with their companions than she had thought.

When Maria fully opened her eyes, she found Banji staring at her with a look of almost horror.

"What?"

"You said nothing would happen to you."

Maria shrugged. "Of course I did. You were just talking about how worried you were about that. I just wanted to reassure you." She couldn't understand why such a simple statement seemed to have Banji so freaked out.

"Um, Maria; no one was talking until you said something." Allo frowned, his eyes shifting between Maria's shoulder and Banji.

"I distinctly heard Banji talking." Maria sighed. "I guess I could have been asleep still and dreaming."

Banji reached for Maria's hand. There was something strange in his eyes, and it made Maria squirm.

Do not fear, jinaria.

Maria yanked her hand from Banji's grip with a squeak.

"I heard you in my mind."

Maria realized that it was evening and the transport had come to a stop. She looked around at the faces of the men staring at her. Her heart was racing and she could hear the blood pounding in her ears. She had to get out of there.

Be calm, Maria. We will figure this out.

Maria wrenched the door of the transport open and jumped out. "Get out of my head you...you...furball!" She slammed the door and stomped off towards the scrubby trees they had decided to camp near.

Banji let her go, knowing she needed time to process what had just happened. By the moons, he needed to process it himself. Never in his entire existence had he believed that he would have a bonded mate.

The *kijani* surveyed the surrounding area. There wasn't much cover: a couple of sickly looking trees, a few boulders scattered about. There was a stone outcrop that provided shelter against the wind and shade for at least part of the daylight hours. The warriors could see an enemy coming long before they were in range and, if push came to shove, the outcrop offered a defensive advantage.

Satisfied that his mate would be safe for the time being, Banji ordered the other warriors to begin setting up camp.

The men climbed out of the transport and started unloading the equipment for their camp. Banji made sure to keep Maria in his line of sight, which is why he ran over Boroff.

"What in the five hells was that all about, *kijani*?" Boroff motioned towards Maria. "How could she know what you were thinking?"

Banji didn't know what to tell the young man because he wasn't even certain himself. Instead, he glared at Boroff until the youth raised his hands in surrender and walked away.

Banji frowned and turned back to the transport. He pulled a bundle of light metallic fabric that would be made into tents from the rear. He turned and ran right into Allo.

"You gave her a mating bite, didn't you? You know that is against the law."

"Are you going to turn me in?" Banji growled.

"That law was created to keep couples from going insane when the woman would be forced to move on."

Banji turned and leaned against the transport. He beat the back of his head against the metallic side. "I only bit her once. I thought the bonding took at least three bites."

Allo shrugged and sat on a nearby rock. "Well, the only bonded pair I know are Megan and Reijo. I heard that it only took two bites for their bond to form."

"Why can't I hear her thoughts?" Banji began to pace after voicing what was really bothering him.

"Who knows?" Allo picked at the tiny leaves of the scrub brush growing from the rocky crag.

"Perhaps humans need a second bite to form a complete bond. Maybe she is mentally stronger than you and is keeping her thoughts from you." He looked up at his friend. "Does it really matter? Would anything change the way you feel about her?"

"Of course not!"

Allo leaned back, looking up at the night sky. One of the two moons was beginning to set while the other remained high, but shadowed. It made for an unusually dark night. Stars littered the sky, many more than could be seen in the bright cities. It made a person feel small because it reminded them of the vastness of the universe.

"Then quit worrying. Think of the odds that you would find a mate at all. You and her were born on different worlds in different galaxies. Even just on her planet alone, there were billions of males that she could have chosen. Call it a miracle, fate...the will of the gods...but the fact remains that the odds of the two of you ever meeting each other let alone having a relationship are incalculable."

"Thanks for the pep talk, Obi Wan," Banji growled.

"Wha...never mind." Allo shook off his confusion; obviously he hadn't been devouring the movies like Banji had because it took him a minute to realize that was an Earth reference. "What I'm trying to say, is I doubt the universe would have gone to this much trouble to get the two of you together if it wasn't going to work out in the end."

Banji sank down to the ground and wistfully looked over at Maria.

"It has to work out, Allo. Now that I have met her, I couldn't survive without her in my life. I realize that what I had before was a half life. But I have tasted real joy for the first time in all my years. Oh I might breathe and go through the motions, but without her, something inside me would be missing. She is my soul."

Allo laughed and made gagging noises. "Blargh…I never knew you could wax poetic. You should probably write that down, I'm not certain you would ever be so eloquent again."

"You better be glad that Akia and I consider you a friend."

"What are you talking about 'a friend'? I'm your best friend and you know it. No one else can put up with your dragon spider shit." Allo just laughed at Banji's glare. "If I ever get all moony-eyed over a female, please just put me out of my misery. You've become way too serious. Quit moping and go talk to your woman."

Banji threw the camp cloth at Allo, knocking him off the rock he was sitting on. "Fine, but that means you get to set up the tents."

"So what's new?"

Banji stood up and offered a hand to Allo. He pulled his friend upright and gave him an awkward hug. "Thanks."

"Hey that's what *best* friends are for you know," Allow said as he walked away waving the bundle of cloth.

Banji looked up at the stars. He wondered briefly if Earth was among one of those twinkling lights or if it was too far away to be seen from Vukas. Shaking his head, he turned away from the vast universe and walked to the woman who had become his world. He was a lucky bastard and he knew it; the rest was just details.

CHAPTER TWENTY-THREE

The light of dawn filtered through the tent opening. Maria's eyes felt crusty and her body ached. She had spent most of the night crying while lying in the Vukasin equivalent of a sleeping bag on the ground, which was an amazing piece of camping equipment. It stretched and conformed to the person that crawled into it and could keep a body warm or cool, depending upon the ambient temperature at the time. When empty it was only about the size of a back pack. Her only real complaint was it didn't provide any cushion against the hard ground.

She didn't even have Banji to curl up to. He had checked on her a few times, but when she refused to talk to him, he gave her space. She had acted like a bitch and she knew it. It just seemed that Vukas was taking over and taking away her choices.

She already agonized over whether or not she should stay with Banji or try to go back to Earth.

It's true she was falling in love with Banji, but she still had doubts. Now she was connected to him in a way that was more intimate than sex. Frankly, it scared the hell out of her. So she did what she normally did when she was scared; she got angry.

Maria rolled over, tucking one arm under her head. She listened in on Banji's thoughts most of the night. He wasn't upset at her. He was worried about her and blamed himself for her outburst. She had gathered that the love bite that he had given her was most likely the cause of this somehow. Banji had berated himself for hours about losing control and how an honorable man would have made sure that it had been Maria's choice.

Maria kind of liked the fact that Banji wanted her so much that he lost control. It amazed her that through the night he never once became angry or blamed her. Banji was unlike any man she had ever met. She could see the capacity for violence in his mind, but it was surrounded by a wall of honorable intentions. No one would ever be able to convince Banji to go against his convictions of what was right. But he wasn't blindly loyal; he questioned everything and made his own decisions from there. He loved fiercely and didn't give his loyalty lightly.

But the most surprising part of Banji was that despite his confident, easygoing demeanor, he was, at his heart, an insecure little boy craving love. Maria began to understand the damage that the lack of women and the subsequent decisions to try to preserve their race had wrought. If a man like Banji didn't feel worthy of love, it meant something fundamental had been broken.

That was Maria's epiphany. Banji needed her. He needed her to show him that he was worthy of being loved. She knew that he loved her, even if he hadn't said the words aloud. Whenever he had looked at her or thought about her, wonder had filled his mind. It made her feel beautiful and desired. The intensity of his emotions swamped her thoughts. She wasn't sure she was worthy of such unconditional adoration, but she also knew that she would be a fool to turn her back on it.

Being able to read Banji's mind still kind of freaked her out. But it helped to settle her heart and her own head. She now knew that Banji was it for her. As long as he was with her, she could make anyplace home. Now she just had to figure out how to apologize to everyone for her behavior last night.

Maria popped her arms out of the top of the sleeping bag and stretched. When she extended her legs, her foot bumped into something large and solid that was lying next to her. Maria froze. No one was supposed to be in the tent with her. She could feel Banji was on the other side of the campsite, just waking.

Whatever was next to Maria's leg moved, and she could hear a rattling sound. It reminded her of the noise an American rattlesnake made on that nature documentary she watched about vipers of the world, but the sound was much louder, and the thing next to her was much, much larger.

Maria's instinct was to burrow deeper under the covers. After all every child knew the monsters couldn't get you if you were under the covers. Unfortunately, Maria was an adult and she knew that she was going to have to deal with the intruder in her tent.

Ever so slowly, Maria inched the sleeping bag down. Her eyes dilated and she quit breathing. Inches from her face was the head of a snake that rivaled a Great Dane for size. Slowly, Maria eyed the creature up and down. She didn't want to make any sudden moves for fear of the thing attacking.

Its body was thick, larger around than the giant snakes she had seen in zoos back home. Its scales were a sandy color with copper markings that reflected metallic light when it undulated closer. The head was larger and wider than a human's, with slitted yellow topaz eyes.

It occurred to Maria that if this snake wanted

to eat her, it could easily. She wondered if it ate its prey whole like snakes back on Earth. She really didn't want to die of suffocation or crushing.

The creature shifted and gently wrapped its coiled body around Maria. It leaned its head in close until it was almost nose to nose with Maria. Then it flicked out its forked tongue and licked Maria on the nose.

Maria's eyes opened wide at the same time her mouth did. She took a deep breath, not realizing she had been holding it in the first place, and screamed.

CHAPTER TWENTY-FOUR

Banji was just waking from a troubled sleep. He still hadn't figured out how he was going to fix things with Maria, but he knew he had to. Sleeping without her in his arms last night had been a form of torture he didn't want to repeat.

Before his mind was fully functioning, he heard Maria cry out in fear. He wrestled out of the sleeping sack and sprinted towards her tent. He didn't care that he was sans shoes and shirt. He didn't even register the pain of hidden stones in the sand on his bare feet. His only thought was to get to Maria.

Banji leapt over the embers of last night's fire. He was quickly joined by the rest of the men with weapons drawn. Their eyes surveyed the campground; nothing seemed out of place. Banji looked over at Daya, who had been on watch. Daya shook his head and mimed that he had seen no one enter.

The men stopped outside of Maria's tent and Banji directed them to surround it. He wanted to make sure that whoever was in the tent with Maria wasn't able to escape before they were able to question them.

Banji took point. He could hear Maria begging for the intruder to not kill her. His canines lengthened and claws burst from his fingers. The phase took him over. His vision sharpened and strength flowed through his limbs. The person threatening her better hope one of the other men reached them first, because he would rend them apart.

Claws shredded through the tent's door as Banji burst through with a battle roar. He was stopped short by snapping fangs, dripping venom and an angry rattle. Eligio yanked Banji out of the tent before the massive viper bit him.

"You idiot, that is a wild shesha serpent. It hasn't been devenomed."

Banji struggled against the medic's hold; he was surprisingly strong.

"I have to get Maria out of there. One bite would kill her."

"Stop and think. I know that the totem animals of each clan are part of the basic education. Use your brain, not just your muscle."

Banji quit struggling. "Are you by chance related to Kavi?"

"Look, the shesha didn't unfurl her hood until you came growling through the tent door. Your actions made her aggressive. She put herself between you…the threat…and Maria."

"Are you saying that thing is trying to defend Maria?"

"Shesha make loving and loyal companions, granted the domesticated ones usually have their venom sacs removed just to be on the safe side. They are a communal animal, and this one seems to be alone. I don't think it is out of the realm of possibility that it was searching for nest mates and decided that it liked Maria."

Eligio looked towards the tent. The serpent had retracted its hood, but it remained coiled around Maria. Every once in a while it would head bump Maria on the shoulder.

"I think she should try to pet it. Use your bond; tell her what it is and what to do."

"If this doesn't work, I'm feeding you to the serpent."

Jinaria….

Banji concentrated hard trying to reach out to Maria. Then he realized that they only had a one-way connection and he wouldn't know if he had reached her or not. He turned to explain to Eligio that they didn't have a full bond yet when he collapsed to his knees, clutching his head.

Banji…please, help me.

It's going to be all right, Maria.

Banji turned down the panicked volume of Maria's thoughts. He concentrated on sending reassuring waves of emotion. Eligio may be right that the serpent didn't want to hurt Maria, but it was still an unpredictable, wild creature.

I think this snake is trying to tenderize me before it eats me. It keeps bumping its head against me.

She just likes you. Eligio thinks you should try to pet her.

Her? How can he tell that this thing is a girl? It's not like you can see a set of boobs on it.

"Maria wants to know how you can tell that it is female."

"She opened a hood when she was acting aggressive. Males don't have a hood."

"Really? I didn't know that. Of course not too many people in the mountains have sheshas as pets…."

Hey! Possible snake kibble over here. Focus please.

You can do this, Maria. Just reach out and touch it. If you feel like it acts aggressively, Daya is on the other side of the tent with a stunner.

Maria tentatively reached for the nearest coil. She gently ran her hand down the coppery scales. She was surprised at how warm the shesha was. Maria had expected the creature to be cold blooded and cool to the touch, like snakes from Earth. The serpent arched its body towards Maria's hand. Emboldened by the reaction, Maria increased the pressure of her touch, running her fingernails over the scales, scratching the shesha like she would a puppy back home.

The shesha closed its eyes and raised it nose in the air while the rattle at the end of its tail wagged back and forth. Maria laughed.

It's working. I think it likes me.

Banji could hear the wonder in his mind. Memories of a few different small furry animals flashed through his mind. The shesha reminded Maria of childhood pets, and he caught a glimpse of her life before Vukas.

The shesha bumped its head under Maria's chin and rubbed its sinuous body across her lap and back. Maria reached up and scratched the creature's chin and she could have sworn the thing panted in contentment like a dog.

Maria decided to take a chance and stood up. The shesha wrapped around her legs and raised its head to Maria's hand, demanding another petting.

"What are we going to call you?"

The shesha just looked at Maria and tilted its head.

"The only snake names I know are all villains." Maria scratched the back of the head, causing the rattle to go crazy. "You just don't seem like much of a villain to me." The serpent's mouth hung open, with its forked tongue lolling to one side. Maria swore that the thing was smiling at her. "You know, back on my planet there was a famous queen who committed suicide by a poisonous snake. Eligio says that you are female...so Cleopatra it is; but I'll call you Cleo for short."

*****

Maria made her way out of the tent about the same time that Banji decided to rush in. All he was getting was vague feelings from Maria and he was worried. Her frightened scream still haunted him.

Neither was really paying attention and they ran right into each other with an "Oomph."

Cleo was right there, forcing herself between Maria and Banji just outside of the tent. Her hood was open, and she was hissing loudly. Dagger-like fangs dripped venom. She snapped at Banji, forcing him to back up.

"No, Cleo!" Maria's sharp reprimand had the giant snake turning towards her. It only partially lowered its hood and rattled its tail. Maria never knew that a reptile was capable of giving puppy-dog eyes.

Banji took a step closer and Cleo turned and bared her fangs again.

Maria got in between Banji and Cleo, moving each time Cleo tried to get around her.

"No, Cleo. Bad…uh, snake."

Cleo hung her head, while Eligio laughed, "You've got a shesha with a lot of personality there." He held out a hand to Cleo, who gingerly slithered up to him, tasting his open palm with her forked tongue. She must have decided that Eligio was all right because she head butted his hand, asking for a scratch. Eligio obliged. "She reminds me of the pet our den instructor kept. I think half the reason he was so successful is because we wanted to play with his shesha."

Maria reached over to stroke her new pet. "You will have to teach me how to take care of her."

"Sure, I'd be happy to."

Eligio smiled up at Maria and Banji felt a pang of jealousy. He was feeling let out. Watching the way she laughed at the antics of Cleo and the easy comradery between her and Eligio made Banji realize that part of him wanted to whisk Maria away so he could have her all to himself.

But she was so beautiful when she laughed, and her smile was reaching her eyes. She was sparkling and bright.

Eligio pet Cleo. "In ancient times, bonding with a wild totem animal would have made you a member of the clan."

"I don't know if I want to be a part of the Tanis clan." Maria remembered that Eligio was part of the Tanis clan. "No offense."

Eligio smiled ruefully. "None taken. I'm not particularly proud to be Tanis at the moment either. But if it is any consolation, despite Cleo here, you wouldn't officially be Tanis. Anyone can tame a wild animal, but a true bonding is rare. In fact I think Reijo's lady is the first to have a confirmed bond in many generations."

Banji walked over to the pair. "If you were truly bonded it would be a psychic connection." He sat next to Maria, which caused Cleo to hiss and rattle at him.

"No, Cleo." The shesha subdued but sulked. "So Megan can talk to those giant cats that are always hanging around?"

"Megan says it is more like feeling their emotions and seeing pictures. The only distinct words she heard was their names."

Cleo forced herself between Banji and Maria and snapped at Banji when he didn't immediately move over.

"I'm beginning to think that maybe I should have her de-venomed like the pets Eligio was talking about." Maria shoved the large serpent to her other side. If Cleo was going to hang around she was going to have to accept Banji as a part of the group.

"No." Maria was surprised when Banji was the one to object.

"I don't want her to hurt you, Banji."

He reached over and caressed her cheek. "I appreciate your concern, but your shesha would make an excellent last line of defense for you and she needs her venom for that."

Maria laid her head on Banji's shoulder and wrapped her arms around his middle for a hug. He was such an amazing man. He always thought about her needs. She vowed to do the same for him.

Maria leaned up and kissed Banji's cheek. Cleo stuck her nose there and flicked her forked tongue between Maria's lips and Banji's face.

Maria was laughing when she put up her hand to deflect her pet's tongue.

Banji wiped his face and muttered, "She is most definitely going to obedience training though."

CHAPTER TWENTY-FIVE

"Am I only the only person who feels like they are in a horror movie?" Maria eyed her surroundings.

People peeked out windows only to hide behind shutters. Businesses closed their doors. The streets were practically deserted.

"I do not know what this 'horror movie' is, but I feel uneasy here." Daya palmed one of his many weapons in his hand. He elbowed the young Boroff. "Keep alert, whelp. I scent trouble."

Cleo rattled in agitation. The feeling of fear hung over the entire town. The sun was bright and the sky clear, yet a gloom made the shadows lengthen.

The group pulled their transport up to the local inn. A stooped old man with silver hair greeted them at the door.

"You've come at a sorry time I'm afraid. But

please come in and rest a bit before you move on." The old man held the door wide for all to pass, but Daya remained outside. Maria knew that he was guarding their backs because of the wariness all of them had as they traveled through the town.

"Elder, what if we wanted to stay for a while?" Banji asked the man.

"Then I would say keep that shesha of yours close." His eyes darted up and down the deserted street. "But if I was carrying such precious cargo," he nodded his head towards Maria, "I would not stay here."

"We have business to attend to before we can move on."

"So be it." The old man shuffled away towards the kitchens. Maria noticed that he dragged his right leg as if it was dead. He stopped and called over his shoulder. "The first two rooms on the second floor are clean and empty. I'll get a couple of more rooms ready if you want."

"Two rooms will be plenty." Banji put a hand in the small on Maria's back to guide her towards the rooms.

The old man nodded and started shuffling again. "I'll have the mid-day meal prepared in about an hour. It will be simple fare, but filling."

Maria turned and smiled at the old man, "Thank you so much for your hospitality."

The elder blushed and then coughed to regain his composure. "M'lady, you would do well to convince your companions that all of you should move on quickly." The inn keeper hastily retreated to the kitchen area.

"I wonder what that is all about."

Banji guided her up the stairs. "I'm sure we will get more information after Daya finishes his reconnaissance."

A rattle was heard at the bottom of the stairs.

"Do you think Cleo will have difficulty with the stairs?"

"I'm sure she will figure it out. She will probably leave to go out hunting shortly anyway." Banji pushed Maria behind him and opened the door. The uneasy feeling the town gave him was getting worse. He quickly searched the quaint room and attached bathing room. He then motioned that Maria could enter.

*****

It wasn't the fanciest place, but it was clean and serviceable. There was a set of doors that led to a balcony instead of a window. The bed was huge by Maria's opinion but was probably an average double for the large Vukasins. Still, it was nicer than anything Maria had slept in for months.

The most important thing was the bathing room though. The medics back at the Tiaret military camp had cleaned her up, but Maria hadn't had a proper bath since her first kidnapping. She flushed thinking of how bad she must have stunk the day Banji was thrown into her cell.

Banji seemed to read her mind. He handed her a large soft cloth. It felt almost like suede, but she had learned in the military camp that it absorbed water like a sponge. It was the Vukasin version of a towel and bathmat all rolled into one thing.

"You can clean up first and I will keep watch. When you are done, I'll have one of the others sit with you so I can take a turn."

Maria caught a picture of her naked and dripping with water from Banji's mind as well as a longing and vulnerability one wouldn't expect from such a masculine man. Maria knew he would never ask for what she saw. She tried to use their new mental connection to send him erotic thoughts. She missed being in his arms.

Banji sucked in a breath and his eyes widened. Maria was pretty sure her thoughts got through, but he still turned away to settle his various weapons on the bed.

"You know," Maria approached him, slowly pulling her tunic over her head. "It really would be more efficient if we bathed together." She tossed the tunic aside and ran a hand up his back.

Banji startled her by turning suddenly and

grabbing her.

"Thank the twin moons, I was afraid what I saw was my own lusty thoughts."

He lifted her up and crushed his lips against hers. Two long strides and he was standing in the door of the bathing room. Maria giggled as he tried to hold her and undress at the same time.

Maria pushed his hands away from his shirt and she slowly began to strip him. She ran her fingers over the taunt muscles of his stomach, causing them to flutter. She pulled the shirt over his head and tossed it aside. It didn't matter that he had to bend forward for her to accomplish the task. She kneaded the muscles of his broad shoulders before pulling him close to her. Her naked breasts pressed into the hard planes of his chest.

Maria's mouth sought to pull them together into one being, and she sighed her denial when Banji broke away from her kiss. He turned long enough to wave his hand in front of a crystal dial to start the water flowing. He adjusted the temperature until steam was soon filling the bathing room.

Banji beckoned Maria towards him and she went, adding a little more roll to her hips to fire him up. The heat certainly flared in Banji's eyes. He grabbed her as soon as she was within reach, but instead of kissing her like Maria thought he would, he turned her around so she faced away from him.

She could feel the heat of his body in her back and his hands blazed a trail and they explored her curves. He cupped her breasts and teased her nipples into hard pebbles. Her moan of pleasure turned into a groan of denial when his hands fell away.

Banji growled in Maria's ear and pressed her to lean forward. In front of her was a simple shelf formed into the wall with a blank space above it. She braced her hands on the shelf and laid her head against the wall. Suddenly all the wall surfaces became reflective. Depending on where she looked, Maria could see her and Banji from almost any angle. She looked directly ahead and caught Banji's eye in the mirror. The intensity staring back at her should have terrified her, but it didn't. While an almost animalistic lust radiated from Banji's mind, it was simply icing over much deeper and stronger emotions.

Banji nipped at her shoulder, his teeth scraping back and forth against her skin.

"You can bite me again. I don't mind," Maria told him breathlessly.

Lust spiked until it was almost overwhelming to Maria.

"*Jinaria*, have no doubt that I will sink my teeth into your beautiful flesh before we are done, but it will not be before I have sunk deep into your warm folds. I want to feel your body shatter around my staff."

"Please, Banji...I need..." Maria pressed her body back against Banji's rigid length.

"I will savor you this time." Banji pulled both of them under the spray of warm water.

Maria watched Banji as he seemed fascinated with the path of a single drop of water that traced its way from her collar bone and over her breast. Banji traced its path with a finger until he palmed her entire breast.

Maria knew that Banji wanted to control the pace of their love making, but there was a large part of her that needed to know she had power over Banji. The trauma nurse in her knew it probably related to the events that occurred during her imprisonment; she would have to face it eventually, but right now she just wanted to feel.

"Come back to me, Maria. They have no place here." Banji's softly whispered command reminded Maria that he was in her head as much as she was in his.

Maria turned from Banji and purposely arched her back to emphasize the curve of her backside. She felt his lust spike and could see his hungry eyes on her in the mirrored surface that surrounded them. She smiled a Mona Lisa smile and pushed her desire across their connection to mingle with his.

Recessed into the side of the shower was what Maria assumed was a soap dispenser. She placed her hand under it and was rewarded with a silky purple foam. She rubbed her hands together and turned back to Banji.

"Let me take care of you tonight."

Banji just nodded as Maria stalked closer to him. She indicated that he should sit on the bench in the shower's corner while she climbed behind him. Maria used the soap to lubricate her movements as she massaged Banji's shoulders. She chuckled as he groaned in ecstasy. Maria had known that he needed to release the stress of the last few days. She loved that she was able to give him this. It allowed her to feel more like a partner in this relationship. She wanted Banji to need her as much as she needed him.

Banji grabbed Maria's hand as it passed over his pectoral muscles. "I will always need you, *jinaria*. You are the only thing that brings meaning to my life. Without you I am no better than a computer that just responds to directives. I need you to truly live." He placed a kiss on the inside of Maria's palm before pulling her into his lap for a deep, soul-searing kiss. "Did touching me arouse you as much as it did me, beautiful?"

"Can't you feel it?" Maria panted.

"I want to hear you say it. Did your hands,"

he kissed her neck, "on my skin," his teeth scraped over her collar bone, "arouse you?" He latched on to her breast, causing her to moan in response. "Say it or I will stop," he challenged against her skin.

Maria held his head to her breast, "Don't you dare. Yes! Yes, it aroused me. Now what are you going to do about it?"

Banji chuckled. He stood, picking Maria up in his arms and passed them both under the water's spray to rinse away the soap. Maria gasped and shook water from her hair, but she didn't let go of Banji. Banji waved his elbow at the controls to turn the water off and marched out of the bathing room with both of them dripping.

He laid Maria on the bed almost reverently. "What do you want, my love?"

Do you really love me? Maria's uncertainty whispered through Banji's mind.

Always and forever.

Tears trailed down Maria's cheeks as she felt the truth of Banji's words and commitment. Women had searched the entire Earth to find something this soul deep and never found it. *Dios*, it had taken Maria traveling to another planet before she found it.

"I want you inside me—where you belong."

Where I belong.... Emotion engulfed Maria's mind until she could no longer tell where Banji stopped and she began. They were one in a way the women of Earth would never be.

Banji traced a finger over Maria's slit. "So wet for me."

"Please, Banji I need you."

That simple plea broke Banji. He thrust home, and their love making quickly shifted from slow and sweet to fast and animalistic.

Maria was thrilled that she was able to make Banji lose control. Their minds were firmly merged together, creating a feedback loop of lost and love that fed and built on each other. Maria held on, digging her nails into Banji's biceps as he held himself above her, thrusting faster and deeper.

Her climax was rapidly approaching, but seemed just out of reach until Banji widened his legs and changed the angle of penetration. One…two…three, and her soul shattered into bright colors.

Banji soon roared his own release. Instinct flowed through him and he couldn't stop the mating bite even if he had wanted to. He tasted her blood on his tongue. He sucked and licked to speed her healing. They then came down from heaven together. He collapsed on the bed, careful not to crush Maria, and pulled their sweat-slicked bodies together.

"So much for the shower." Maria smiled.

"Give me a minute and I will be more than happy to try all of this again," Banji mumbled into

Maria's shoulder.

She playfully slapped his arm and was about to respond when her stomach growled loudly.

Banji chuckled. "Perhaps we should feed you first." His gaze turned serious and he gently brushed a lock of hair from Maria's face. "You didn't panic."

For a moment Maria didn't understand what Banji meant. Then it hit her; he had been over her, caging her in, and not once did what the Tanis did to her intrude. She didn't have a single prickle of anxiety.

She smiled and reached up and kissed Banji, "I think our connection made it easier for me. I was in your mind; I knew that no matter how rough it got between us that you would never hurt me." She caressed his cheek. "Thank you."

Banji groaned and rolled over. He stood next to the bed and reached for his pants. Maria admired the view of his beautifully sculpted ass and fought the urge to grab it.

"If we don't get downstairs soon, the only thing that we will be eating is each other," Banji replied out loud to Maria's thoughts, but he projected that he wouldn't mind so much if that happened.

Maria choked on a laugh. "I need sustenance before we go another round."

Banji tossed her tunic at her. "So cover up the temptation."

"No self-control, huh?" Maria obliged and pulled the tunic over her head and stood to locate her pants.

Banji grabbed her and kissed her until her knees turned to jelly. "Absolutely none where you are concerned.

CHAPTER TWENTY-SIX

Maria and Banji finally made it downstairs. They found Allo, Eligio, Boroff, and Daya gathered in the common room that doubled as the dining room. Cleo was curled up next to the fireplace, which was happily burning, though Maria was surprised that the flames had a green tint.

Banji saw Maria staring at the flames. "The people in this area use a mixture of shesha waste and the wood of the *d'han* bush, since the land rarely supports trees. The mixture burns for many hours, but it is also very high in magnesium which turns the flames green."

Maria shook her head and laughed. "You sure know how to ruin a magical alien world experience for a girl."

Banji placed a hand in the small of Maria's

back and guided her to the dining tables the other men were already sitting at.

Boroff scented the air, while Allo openly stared at the juncture of Maria's neck and shoulder.

"You mated her!" the young Boroff practically shouted. "The mating bite is illegal."

Daya smacked the whelp in the back of the head. "Don't be rude."

Boroff glared at Daya while Maria covered the mating bite with her hand. All the men could tell that they had made her uncomfortable. Daya glared right back at Boroff and motioned with his chin at Maria. Boroff looked at her and finally noticed that she had shrunk into herself and was red with embarrassment.

The young man looked down and mumbled, "Sorry. I was just surprised."

Banji sat down and pulled Maria into his lap, hugging her close. "Ghaleb dissolved that law when the council voted to allow females the choice to stay with a single male or not. It was declared that the choice of forming a mating bond was between the man and the woman involved and that the government had no place in it. Not that it is any of your business, but we had already started the mating bond before here."

The brewing political debate was halted by the arrival of the inn keeper with steaming bowls of stew and dark crusty bread. As he said, it was simple fair, but as far as Maria was concerned it was a gourmet meal. For months she starved on the meager meals the guards gave the prisoners once a day where she had been held. When she regained consciousness in the military encampment after her rescue, she had been given nutritionally dense field rations to help bring her body back to where it needed to be. While filling, those things were basically tasteless.

The inn keeper placed a bowl and small loaf of bread in front of Maria first, and she took a deep breath, filling her lungs with the spicy scent of the stew and yeasty bread. She tore off a chunk of bread and dipped it into the broth in her bowl. She popped the moistened bit of bread into her mouth and moaned in pleasure as the taste spread across her tongue.

She opened her eyes to find all of the men staring at her, spoons stopped midway to their mouths.

She raised her hand to cover her mouth, which was still full of food. "Sorry, it is just so delicious."

The inn keeper chuckled, "Well I can't say that many have had the same reaction, but thank you." He turned to Banji and held out a large egg that nearly took both hands to hold. "I brought this for your shesha, if you don't mind."

Banji nodded, and the old man laid the egg near the giant serpent.

"That kind of looks like an ostrich egg," Maria said once she swallowed.

"It is the egg of a *kitack*, a kind of reptilian bird hybrid."

"A missing link," Maria said between mouthfuls.

Banji nodded and the conversation stalled. The only sounds heard were those of hungry travelers eating, punctuated by the crack and slurp of Cleo's meal.

Maria was nearly finished with her bowl of stew when her vision started to tunnel and her limbs felt thick. She tried to get her mouth to work but it was quickly becoming more difficult to control. It suddenly pierced the fog of her mind that she had been drugged. She tried to look at Banji to warn him, as she heard her companions fall one by one.

Banji!...

Darkness stole her vision and she would swear that she heard the inn keeper crying and asking them to forgive him.

CHAPTER TWENTY-SEVEN

Banji groaned. His head felt like a ghost lion was trying to claw its way out of his brain. He tried to raise his hands to rub his temple, only to discover that they were tied securely behind his back. He pulled but could not free either one of his hands; the bonds were tight and the material used to bind them strong. He cracked an eye open and looked around. He seemed to be in a store room. Dry goods and various processed food containers lined the walls.

A moan sounded behind him and Banji shifted until he could see where it had come from. He was relieved to see his three male companions. Daya was already starting to come to, but Allo, Eligio and Boroff remained deathly still. Banji had recovered sooner because his body had built up a mild immunity to many commonly used drugs, thanks to his training with Ghaleb's spy master Kavi. The fact that Daya regained consciousness nearly as quick brought up questions about his background that Banji would explore later.

Banji searched their makeshift prison for Maria, but she wasn't there. He reached out across their bond and was met with silence. He had to assume that she was still under the influence of whatever had knocked them out—because the alternative was unacceptable.

"That *frexing* buzzard raptor drugged us." Daya pushed himself upright. "When I get my hands on him, I am going to kill him."

"We need answers first. Maria is gone." Banji imbued his voice with authority, letting Daya know that he couldn't harm the inn keeper until after he had been questioned.

Daya strained against his bonds, but they held just as tightly as Banji's did. It was possible that Banji could dislocate his shoulder and contort himself to get his hands in front of him where he could possibly remove his bonds with his teeth. It was a painful process and, more importantly, it left whichever side he dislocated weak, even after popping the shoulder joint back into place. They had no way of knowing what they were going to face in the coming days, and Banji didn't want to be at a disadvantage.

"Daya can you maneuver over here?"

"I'll have to crawl over Allo, but yeah.

Why?"

"If we can get back to back, maybe we can untie each other's hands."

Banji moved toward Daya, while Daya made his way to Banji.

"There should be a small knife in my belt," Daya said to Banji. "If you can get to it, cut through my bonds. It will be faster than trying to figure out how to get out of them blind."

Banji felt around Daya's belt, noticing a multitude of small hidden pockets as he searched. He was really going to have to have a frank discussion about where Daya came from when this was all over.

Soon Banji's fingers brushed over the hilt of a small knife. Using fingers that were going numb from their tight binds, he fiddled with the knife until he could pull it free. Clumsy fingers dropped the knife to the ground.

"Dragon spider shit."

Banji felt around the ground searching for the knife. He found it when it nicked his finger. Feeling his way up the blade until he reached the hilt, Banji was able to grasp the knife firmly in his hand.

If was awkward cutting through Daya's binding, but soon the man's hands were free with a final rip. Daya took the knife from Banji and made short work of the bindings on Banji's hands. While Banji rubbed blood back into his fingers, Daya started to cut away the bonds on their legs.

"Five hells, how many layers of shipping straps did he use on us?"

Their captor had used bands that would expand or contract when delivered an electrical charge. On Vukas, it was mostly used to secure goods being shipped from one place to another. Just about every household had some.

When they were free, Banji checked on Allo and Boroff. Both men were breathing evenly and had strong pulses, so Banji knew that they had just been knocked out. He was relieved that they were alive.

Banji reached for Maria once more and still found nothing. His body tingled as it tried to force a shift. Age old instincts to protect his mate rose to the surface. He had to get himself back under control before he lashed out at any male near him.

"If they harm Maria my rage will know no bounds." Daya recoiled from Banji's glittering eyes; the beast was very near the surface.

The inn keeper took that moment to enter the storage area. His gasp of surprise was cut off when Daya launched himself at the man and pinned him against the door.

"Please don't kill me," the inn keeper croaked out. "I had no choice."

Banji's feral growl leeched all color from the older man's face.

"If I were you, I would start talking—and quickly. My friend here has little patience where his mate is concerned."

"M...m...mate? I didn't know. I swear." The inn keeper collapsed into tears.

"Let's start with what did you dose us with?"

"The nectar of the sleep flower." The inn keeper said between sobs. "You should have slept for at least another few hours."

Daya released the pathetic man and laid a hand on Banji's arm, trying to calm him. "Maria received the same dose we did. Give it a few hours before you lose it."

Banji pulled in a calming breath. The sleep flower was the primary ingredient in the injectable they had used to collect the women. So he knew that it shouldn't harm Maria. Knowing she was most likely just unconscious helped him to get himself under control.

"Pull him out into the common room and secure him. Lock down the building. I don't want any interruptions."

Daya turned and grabbed the old inn keeper by the collar of his shirt and dragged him out.

"Want me to start questioning him, *kijani*?"

Banji reached for Allo's prone body and lifted him onto his shoulder. "That's fine. Just make sure you keep him alive."

"Does he have to be in one piece?"

"Depends on how cooperative he is."

It took a moment for the implications of Banji's orders to register with the inn keeper. The old man started crying again, but he walked out the door under his own power instead of having Daya drag him out.

Banji carried his friend to the nearest bedroom and laid him on the mattress. He went back and did the same with Boroff. He knew he was stiff from his short time laying on the floor; if his friends were going to be out a few more hours, the comfort of the bed would make getting moving again easier.

Banji systematically searched each room and out building at the inn. All he found was a lot of dust and disuse. The inn hadn't been used for months most likely. Maria wasn't found in any of the rooms. He had hoped that the inn keeper hadn't had time to move her yet, but that didn't seem to be the case. As best he could tell, he and Daya had been out less than an hour, so Maria couldn't be too far away.

When checking the out buildings, Banji noticed that all traces of their visit had been removed or hidden. Their vehicle had been buried under tarps. Even Cleo was missing.

Banji was almost through the last storage building when he heard a loud knocking and scraping. He pulled the small pulse gun he kept hidden in his boot. Slowly he made his way around the huge stacks of junk that littered the space. Towards the back he found a large metal box that was rocking side to side and scraping along the floor.

Banji tried reaching for Maria once more, hoping that it was her trying to fight her way out of the container, but he was still only getting silence. Either the inn keeper could sever their bond, something he had never heard of occurring, or it wasn't Maria in the box.

Banji approached the box cautiously. It had a simple latch and didn't appear to be locked on the outside. Banji flipped the latch and stepped behind another pile of boxes, his gun at the ready.

The lid of the box exploded open and an angry shesha sprang forth, landing in a pile of coils with its rattle going and hood unfurled. It flicked its tongue and scented Banji, turning on him with a hiss.

Banji held up his hands and stayed very still. The markings on the hood identified this animal as Maria's Cleo; he would hate to have to kill it.

Cleo lunged at him, snapping her jaws in front of Banji's face with venom dripping from her fangs, but she didn't bite him. She flicked her tongue at him and then settled in front of him. She still had her hood opened, but her rattle wasn't as erratic and angry.

Cleo looked all around Banji, twining her

body around his legs. He knew she was looking for Maria.

"She's not here, girl. They took her away." He gingerly reached out to pet the top of the shesha's head. "But we will get her back. I promise."

With Cleo still tucked under his hand, the pair headed back towards the inn. Cleo stopped and scented the air, then started herding Banji away from the inn. She was insistent that he follow her. Near the main road a few buildings over, Cleo started slithering in circles. Banji could see the tell-tale signs of a hover motor taking off and, when the wind shifted, he smelled the faint scent that he would know anywhere…Maria.

Most likely this was where they loaded her into a transport to take her away. Banji scanned the area, but whoever did this was long gone. The windows of the residents remained firmly shut. It was doubtful any of them would help even if they saw something. Banji called on all of his tracking skills to give him a clue. Only a few acceleration marks pointed him in a western direction.

"Come on, Cleo. Let's see if the inn keeper can tell us anything."

*****

"I don't have a lot for you, *kijani*. I can tell you it was the Tanis, and the inn keeper claims to have saved our lives."

Banji kneeled in front of the bloodied inn keeper. A flash a regret at the old man's rough treatment was pushed out of his mind. The compassion was Maria's influence, but right now he had to be the cold-calculating spy if they had any hope of finding her.

"Why?"

"I had no choice." The inn keeper spat blood at Banji's feet.

"Everyone has a choice." Banji's voice was flat and cold; his eyes held no emotion. "You chose to take my mate from me."

"I didn't know she was your mate. I just thought she was…."

Banji grabbed the front of the man's shirt and twisted, choking off his sentence. "I'd choose your next words very carefully. And if I think you are lying, I will feed you to Cleo."

The serpent raised itself up at the sound of its name. A low hiss followed the opening of its hood. Any desert dweller knew those were signs that the creature was prone to attack.

"Please…I don't care what you do to me. I had to do it." New tears streaked down the old man's face. "They said it was the only way they would give me back my Kalani."

"Who is Kalani?"

"My daughter…they have my daughter."

"Well dragon spider shit," Daya exclaimed from the chair he had been lounging in.

"I need to know everything." Banji's eyes bored into the old inn keeper.

CHAPTER TWENTY-EIGHT

Maria woke to a pounding head and bound hands. She pushed herself up into a sitting position, cursing colorfully in Italian.

"Here's some water. If you promise not to fight I will untie your hands."

Maria turned to see an older woman who kind of looked familiar. She couldn't promise not to fight but she needed her hands free, so Maria just nodded. It wasn't her fault that the woman took that for acceptance.

Maria took a long drink of water. It wasn't very cold, but at least it was wet and helped with the dry-mouth feeling being drugged caused. She handed the canister back to the woman.

"Thanks." Maria looked around her new prison. Unlike the stronghold, this one wasn't carved out of natural rock. It was all metal and smooth blocks of stone. Maria rubbed her temples. Her head ached but she needed it clear to think of a way to escape. "This kidnapping business is getting really old," Maria grumbled.

The older woman seemed surprised at that. "Just how many times have you been taken?"

"What's your name?"

"I'm called Kalani."

"I'm Maria. This is my third kidnapping…the fourth time I have been 'taken' if you count my temporary rescue."

"You are one of the women from Earth aren't you?"

Maria nodded. She didn't see a point in hiding it since she was obviously not Vukasin.

"I bet that makes you go for a high price at the auction. You are the first Earth woman they have been able to get their hands on as far as I know."

Maria grabbed the woman. "What auction?"

The woman pulled out of Maria's hands and sneered, "Don't you know? The New Tanis Empire has decreed that any male with enough credits is guaranteed a woman."

"That's barbaric!" Maria narrowed her eyes at the woman in front of her. "Why are you still here?"

Kalani shrugged, "I was deemed too old for

the auction. So instead I get to meet all of the poor souls those bastards bring in. Evidently the women are calmer when met with another female."

"Why are you helping them?"

"Do you think I have a choice?" Kalani leaned against the wall of their cell. "It will go easier for you once you realize you don't have a choice either."

"There is always a choice," Maria stated fiercely.

Kalani smiled ruefully. "May the gods protect you then."

*****

"Reijo, I need reinforcements and I need them yesterday." Banji paced in front of the holo-image of his commanding officer and friend.

"I understand that you want Maria back, but I just don't have the manpower to lend you, Banji."

Banji knew that Reijo had to think about the big picture of the civil war as a whole, but honestly he didn't give a damn about that with Maria missing. As the hours passed with him unable to connect to her, his worry grew exponentially.

"I'm not going to lie and tell you that my primary objective isn't Maria, but it is more than that. The people of this town are terrified. The Tanis elites have repeatedly swooped in, taking whatever they want." Banji pulled at his hair, "Five hells,

Reijo, you heard my report about the inn keeper's daughter."

"I sympathize with the man, but trading one woman in hopes of retrieving another...."

"He's a father that loves his child. What would you be willing to do if it had been Abby?"

Reijo sighed and his image wavered. "This man helped abduct your mate and yet you are advocating for him?"

"We both know that enemy and ally isn't black and white. Blame it on Maria's compassion, if you want. These people are as much victims as the Earth women are. If it had been my child, I can't say that I wouldn't have tried to do the same." Banji pushed on when Reijo would have interrupted. "This village is unique. It had a higher percentage of female births than any other area that I know of. When Ghaleb and the council abolished the law forcing women to rotate between males and giving them a choice, this entire area rejoiced. Many of their daughters decided to come home, and families were restored—at least until the Tanis swooped in and stole them away. These are our people and they need our help and protection."

"I think you may have missed you calling in politics, Banji." Reijo chuckled. "Alright, I'll see what I can do, but it is going to take time."

"Troop movements always do."

"I'm going to assume that you will be mounting a rescue mission on your own, right?"

"I won't let her suffer in their hands, Reijo. You can't ask that of me. They have already had her a day and I still can't reach her."

Reijo's image ran an agitated hand through his hair. "We both know that may be because she is dead, Banji."

"She is not dead!" Banji growled. "I would have felt it here," he thumped his chest, "if she had passed to the worlds beyond."

Reijo just stared at his friend silently for a moment then sighed. "Just don't get yourself killed. I still have need of you."

Reijo ended the transmission and the holo-image winked out.

"I can't believe you aren't going to punish the old man." Allo stepped into the common room at the inn. The team had taken over the inn as a base for their operation.

"I didn't say I wasn't going to punish him; I said I wouldn't kill him because I understand why he did what he did. But we can't trust him, so he stays locked up until the troops get here. The justice system can have him after that."

"You are more lenient than I would have been if she had been my mate."

Banji didn't respond; he was getting tired of

215

people assuming he would just kill the inn keeper. Hadn't they seen enough destruction and death? He would have laughed at the fact that he, one of the empire's best spies and assassins, was getting tired of death, but being with Maria made him want a real life with a future. Maybe that was why he spared the inn keeper, or maybe he spared him because it was what Maria would have done.

CHAPTER TWENTY-NINE

"Have you gathered the town folk, Allo?"

Allo snapped to attention; it was his superior officer talking to him now, not his friend. "Yes, *kijani*. Though they weren't happy about it."

Banji walked out the door of the inn and headed to the town square. There he found a crowd of grumbling men. He hoped that he could get through to them because his men were greatly outnumbered. Even untrained masses could overwhelm trained soldiers with large enough numbers.

In the center of the square was an obelisk— probably a monument to some important individual or event. Banji climbed up on its base to use as a stage. He surveyed the crowd, making sure to hold eye contact with any who challenged him until they averted their eyes.

"Good men, I am here to tell you that war is

upon us," Banji projected out over the crowd.

"Tell us something we don't know," a voice in the back yelled.

"War is upon us, and the time has come to choose which side you will be on. I know that the Tanis have used you and stolen that which is most precious to you."

"How do we know that Ivailo would be any different? The elite never consider the common people," a large man with a weathered face challenged from the front of the crowd.

"What is your name, sir?" Banji looked the man in the eye.

The man started to fidget under Banji's intense stare but soon got himself under control. He uncrossed his arms and stood at attention. "I am called Korose."

"Korose, I will not lie to you. Ghaleb Ivailo often forgets that he is dealing with living people, but he is not intentionally cruel, and he truly cares about the populace. Did he not give your daughters back?" Banji addressed that last line to the entire crowd.

"Why should we believe you? You are obviously an elite yourself, even if you dress as a mercenary. Plus, I heard you are keeping old Lorauq prisoner."

Before Banji could form a response, soul-searing pain flashed through his mind. He grabbed his head and collapsed with a scream. Bright lights and flashing pieces of metal raced through his mind. He could feel knives slicing his body open. He knew that he was sharing Maria's experiences, but his body couldn't handle the over-stimulation and reacted as if he was having a seizure. His men rushed the obelisk, pushing away the crowd.

They ignored the cries of, "What's wrong with him?" as they held their convulsing friend. His face and hands kept morphing back and forth between his phased state and his daily appearance. He had to get control. Brick by mental brick he built a wall to push back the connection.

It seemed like an eternity but was probably only a few minutes when Banji's body finally called down with an anguished cry of "Maria." It took a few more moments before Allo and Daya sat him upright.

"Are you all right?"

"I had to shut her out, Allo." Banji grabbed his friend and fought back tears. "By the moons, I shut her out."

"Does he need a medic?" Korose asked.

Allo turned to answer the man, but Banji pushed himself up and stood before the crowd. "They have my mate and by the gods they are hurting her."

Banji didn't understand everything he received through their bond. He wasn't sure exactly what was going on, but it felt like Maria was being tortured. It was possible that they were attempting to extract information. If that was the case, they would most likely kill her once they figured out she had no knowledge of troop movements or orders. They had to find her—and fast.

Banji allowed a small crack in the wall of his mind. He needed to function, but he couldn't stand the thought of Maria being all alone while they tortured her. Even that small crack had pain radiating through it. He poured love and strength through the connection and a plea for her to live until he could get to her. He hoped she could feel him there with her. "I no longer have the luxury of trying to convince you to help us. Either you will or you won't. I couldn't give dragon spider shit either way at the moment. I'm going to go get my mate and I am going to kill every one of those bastards that get in my way." Banji's eyes blazed, "So if you won't help, then stay out of my way."

The crowd murmured about mating bonds and who was the enemy. Banji no longer cared. He turned to prepare to leave when a massive hand stopped him. Banji whipped around with a growl; his phase state was close to the surface.

Korose help up his hands. "I was never

trained as a soldier because I couldn't phase, but no one knows the lands around here better than I do."

Banji nodded and Korose fell in step next to him.

"Is this only about your mate or will you help us get our people back as well?"

"I will get my mate or die trying. The *Khalon* is sending troops here to hopefully rescue your people. They should be here in a few days." Banji looked over the three men he had brought with him.

Korose's shoulders fell. Once again the commoner had to wait in line behind the elite.

Banji saw the defeat in the one man who seemed to be reaching out to help. He couldn't make any real promises; the odds were stacked against them.

"Our numbers are small. We can't rescue everyone. But I promise we will free everyone we can until the others get here to help."

"You are honest and I can accept that."

"Good. You know my mate made me promise to rescue as many females from the Tanis as possible. That was actually why we were here, to gather information to plan a rescue." Banji didn't know why he was telling Korose so much. Maybe he recognized that this area needed some hope. Banji turned. "Allo, take Korose and figure out where we should start. Wherever they are keeping Maria is west of here."

"What are you going to do?"

"I'm going to go light a fire under our illustrious *Khalon's* ass."

"You are going to get Megan after him aren't you?" Allo grinned.

"Yup."

CHAPTER THIRTY

Maria ignored the other woman's glare as she searched their cell. Smooth stone and metal walls made it unlikely that she would find a makeshift weapon, but she had to make sure. As she searched, she turned her mind toward connecting with Banji. The drug they had used to knock her out was still in her system, so her mind was still a bit fuzzy. The accompanying headache made it almost impossible to concentrate. She also had no idea what kind of distance their connection could function over. So she kept trying.

Maria's eyes were closed as she tried to find the mental thread that connected her and Banji. She heard Kalani scramble away from the door just before the locks disengaged. Maria turned and opened her eyes.

One of the men from her nightmares was standing inside the door.

"I see the Tanis are still using substandard

help, Krac."

Maria's bravado just enraged the oversized goon. She watched as his phase rippled across his skin. He growled and, she could see the muscle in his jaw twitching as he ground his teeth together. It looked like he was fighting with himself to maintain control. Back in the valley prison, he had only shifted when he wanted to or when he was told to. What had changed in the last few days?

When Krac got himself under control, he sneered at Maria. "I don't care what Sta'ling says this time. This is all your fault. I will have a taste of you before they sell you."

Maria almost threw up at the thought of that beast of a man's hands on her, though she did wonder what was supposed to be her fault. Instead, she hid her fear behind sharp words. "A real man doesn't have to force himself on a woman." Maria pointedly looked at Krac's crotch. "Oh, that's right…you never were a real man were you?"

Krac shifted into his phased form, though it seemed out of proportion compared to the last time Maria had seen it. He charged Maria and grabbed her by the neck, lifting her up in a terrible act of a déjà vu.

Maria knew it was useless to try and pry his grip from her neck. Instead, she kicked and punched, praying to land some blow that would make him drop her. As darkness crept into her vision; Maria balled up her fist for one last swing. She was aiming for his temple, hoping to stun him even a little bit, but Maria was no warrior and her aim was terrible. She hit him in the neck instead.

Krac's body seized as if an electrical jolt went through him, and he tumbled to the ground like a felled oak. He and Maria lay on the ground, his hand still around her throat as wide, frozen eyes stared at her with hate.

Kalani quickly came over and helped Maria pry Krac's fingers from her bruised throat.

"*Che diavolo è successo?*" Maria fell back into Italian.

"What?"

Maria rubbed her throat and concentrated on repeating her question, "What happened?"

"He didn't have his battle collar on," Kalani stated as if that explained everything. Maria was going to have some questions for Banji when she could finally reach him.

Kalani pulled Maria up and they both looked at the open cell door. Maria knew that she couldn't force the other woman to leave, but she wasn't going to pass up this opportunity for escape.

Maria rushed to the door and looked out to see if there were other guards about. The hall was empty. They would have to hurry because Maria knew from experience that they were most likely being monitored. Maria felt Kalani at her back; evidently the woman decided to take a chance as well.

They both crept out of the cell.

Maria whispered, "I don't suppose you know the way out of here?"

"Head to the left, there should be a door that leads to another hall. If we stay to the right we should eventually find an exit. It was the way they brought me and the others in weeks ago."

Maria quickly made her way down the hall. "How many others?"

"All of the women in my entire village. I was the oldest woman there; the others were all auctioned off and are gone."

Maria reached back and squeezed Kalani's hand. "We will find and rescue everyone we can."

The pair made it down the hall; all of the other cells in their hall were empty. They ducked out of sight as a shadow passed across the window of the door they needed to take. After a few tense minutes, Maria slowly opened the door and peered around the crack. As best she could tell the hall was empty. She slowly eased her way into the new area. She saw a bisecting hall a half dozen doors down. Kalani had said to stay to the right.

Maria ran quickly to the intersection with

Kalani close behind. She briefly glanced into the rooms they passed to make sure that no one was in them. They had moved from a holding area to a medical wing. Maria remembered many of the devices she saw from her time in the valley prison.

Maria stopped at the intersection to check around the corner when she heard Kalani's muffled scream behind her. Maria quickly turned to see the woman squirming in the arms of one of the Tanis guards.

Maria dashed to the left of the guard, hoping to maneuver around him, only to find more guards behind him. She reversed course, making only a few feet before skidding to a stop. She was surrounded. *Madre di dios.* For a planet that was supposedly dying there seemed to be no end to the Tanis manpower.

"I want her alive." Maria shivered; she knew that voice. She had woken up screaming because of that voice. The Doctor…no, she had learned in the Tiaret military camp that the man she had referred to as the Doctor was actually Sta'ling "The Butcher" Tanis. He was here. The question was why?

Maria dashed under the arms of the first guard who tried to grab her. She was working strictly on survival instinct, and it was telling her to get away any way she could. Unfortunately, greater strength and greater numbers beat out her bites and kicks. She tried the nifty little paralyzing trick she discovered on Krac, but when she punched the guard in the neck she nearly screamed in pain as her fist connected with something metal and broke her hand.

In the end she was restrained by two of the guards and hauled over to Sta'ling. He grabbed her chin with bruising fingers and forced her to look into his cold eyes.

"You have caused me more trouble than you are worth, female."

Maria spit on his face.

"I was going to send you to auction where you would only have to deal with the whims of one master." Sta'ling wiped the spittle from his face as it turned into something demonic. "But now when I am done with you, I will send you to the pit and let the beasts fight over you. Perhaps we will even take wagers on how long you will last."

Sta'ling started to turn away when he noticed the neatly scarred mating bite. He ripped the neck of Maria's tunic away so he could confirm it was what he thought it was. Maria fought against her guard's hold as her torn shirt threatened to expose her.

An evil chuckle escaped him. "This is too perfect. If what they say is true, your mate will feel every degradation and humiliation." Sta'ling grinned. "I wonder how long it will take to drive him mad."

"My mate will kill you," Maria growled through clenched teeth.

"Take her to exam room three." Sta'ling waved away the guards holding Maria.

"What about this one?" Another guard brought Sta'lin's attention back to Kalani.

"I should just kill her for her insolence. But," Sta'ling tapped his chin, "we did promise her father that we would send her back if he provided a replacement." A calculating gleam flashed in Sta'lin's eyes. "The Tanis Empire should always keep its promises."

"Yes, sir!" intoned the guards.

"Take her out into the desert in a transport, at least a day's walk from here. No food, no water. I'll be generous and let her keep the clothes she is wearing." Sta'ling smiled at Kalani. It wasn't a nice smile; it was malevolent. "Your village is about a four-day walk from this base or you could voluntarily return to servitude here."

"I would rather take my chances with the shesha and buzzard raptors than return here."

"So be it." Sta'ling dismissed the guards. As they dragged the women off in opposite directions, he called out one last command. "Oh, before you release the village woman, have her flogged for her disobedience."

"You monster! You are going to kill her!"

Maria thrashed trying to get to Kalani, but her guards just held her tighter. Kalani gave her a wan smile and waved goodbye. It killed Maria to see the defeat and acceptance in the other woman's eyes.

Sta'ling walked away without so much as a backwards glance. Maria's guards literally dragged her to the exam room their boss specified. She had already once experienced the horrors found in those rooms; she had no desire to do so again.

She pleaded with the guards, but like most of the Tanis she met during her captivity, they seemed brainwashed into believing that females were somehow subhuman. Might makes right and all of that other misogynistic bullshit. Never had Maria cursed the fact that she had always been a girly girl until now. She vowed that if she made it out of this that she would force Banji to teach her how to defend herself, or maybe Megan would do it since everyone had heard the stories of how she defeated an opponent three times her size before surviving the stupid *Mate Avi Keiger* the council forced her into performing and winning the blessing of the gods.

Each step brought them closer to her worst nightmare. And with each step, Maria became more agitated. She bit and scratched, screamed and cried. She didn't care that she had lost all of her bravado and her terror was showing through.

Somewhere along the line, one of the guards

had grabbed her legs to keep her from kicking them; the other had his arm wrapped around her upper body, pinning her arms down. As they marched down the hall, her struggles had let her slip a little in the grip of the man who held her arms. She wiggled a little more and was able to free an arm. With as much force as she could muster, she jabbed her elbow into his diaphragm, knocking the wind from him.

The move was so unexpected that he nearly dropped her. The man who held her feet lost his grip when she slipped, and she kicked him in the nose. The man who still held her upper body roared in anger and spun her around.

She could see in his eyes that she had pushed him too far. What was with these Tanis males? They were so quick to lose their control. When his hand whipped out and grabbed her throat, slamming her to the ground, she was certain she had crossed the line.

The murderous look in his eyes should have frightened her. She didn't want to die after all. Even if death would be easier than anything Sta'ling had planned.

Darkness tunneled her vision as her brain was starved of oxygen. She watched as the guard's companion tried to calm him down and pull him off of her. He yelled at the man choking the life out of her that they were told she was to be taken alive.

That last comment seemed to pierce the man's rage, and his fingers released Maria's neck. She took an instinctual ragged breath. Her life was saved, but the darkness still stole her consciousness.

CHAPTER THIRTY-ONE

Maria woke up naked in the cold, sterile exam room. They had strapped her tightly down on the metal table. Most of the devices were automated; Sta'ling could control them from a distance. The man was fascinated with how much a body and mind could endure, but he hated actually getting his hands dirty.

A great mechanic beast lowered from the ceiling. It seemed almost alive and evil. This was something new. Before the machines just restrained her to allow the guards to rape her. Or they used various needled to harvest tissue for experiments. Once Sta'ling had subjected her to various shocks and stabs to gauge her pain tolerance. But the thing hovering over her was large enough that it could cover her entire body if it so chose. A multitude of mechanical arms stretched out like a bloated spider ready to capture its prey.

Maria could barely turn her head in the restraints, but she looked to the observation window and saw Sta'ling smirking back at her. He wouldn't walk in until the procedure was done for fear of bodily fluid marring his pristine clothing.

"Get on with it, *bastardi*."

"Patience," Sta'lin's voice echoed through the exam room with a tinny whine. "This procedure is more involved than the others we performed on you." The mechanic spider flipped tools and whirred into different positions with every new command Sta'ling entered. "This surgical unit could perform every necessary task quickly and efficiently, but that is counterproductive to this experiment. Thus far I have relegated my studies to the males. Most are easily broken." Sta'ling sighed. "Such a disappointment."

Sta'ling sent a metal arm, equipped with a scalpel, to stab Maria's broken hand. She bit the inside of her cheek, forcing herself not to cry out.

"You know I was angry will Bel when he insisted that I oversaw this operation. I only agreed after he guaranteed that I would be able to continue my experiments. Inviting the public to watch has turned decidedly profitable." Sta'ling stabbed Maria again. "But despite the credits, it has still been a waste. I'm looking for the perfect predator…. He has to be deadly, but calculating and cunning. Vukasin men all break at some point. Though the ones with intimate partners do seem to last a little longer than the others. Why is that, do you suppose?"

Sta'ling used a cauterizing laser to burn Maria's shoulder. She couldn't help the cry of pain that escaped her throat. Sta'ling stared down at Maria.

"I am waiting on your answer." His hand hovered to send another burn of pain.

"Love...love sustained them and gave them strength."

The Butcher tapped his chin. "Interesting hypothesis. Though I don't understand how a few simple chemical reaction in the brain would affect the fortitude of an individual."

"Of course you can't understand the power of love, you emotionless bastard," Maria hissed.

Sta'lin's face screwed up in rage and he buried the scalpel into Maria's thigh before composing his features into the calm mask that hid the insane monster.

"You really ought to feel privileged; I don't share my work with just anyone. So a little more respect if you please. As I was saying, I was upset that time would be taken away from my natural choice of subject. After all, women are physically weaker than males, plus they tend to be quite emotionally unstable."

Maria wanted to snort at that statement. *Pot calling the kettle black*, she thought.

"Imagine my shock when you and a few other female subjects surprised me with your mental fortitude. You survived pain and humiliation that often broke the males in my care. You continued to fight long after it was obvious that it was futile." Sta'lin's voice raised in pitch; he was angry that his original conclusions might be wrong, and it was tearing at his control. "How is it that the weaker sex is somehow stronger?" He practically screamed that last question.

"There is a saying on my planet: 'the female of the species is more deadly than the male.'" Maria knew she was provoking him but she didn't care.

Surprisingly, Sta'ling ignored her outburst and continued on his rant. "This was important to my research. I wanted to expand to other female test subjects, but they shut me down because the females were necessary for their plans. Control the females and you control the planet."

Sta'ling began to frantically pace almost as if Maria was forgotten there strapped to the table. Not that Maria minded. As long as he was occupied with his crazy rants, he wasn't hurting her. She did concentrate on what he was saying because she didn't think that he realized just how much of Bel's plans he was revealing. Of course that only helped if

Banji got her out of here before they killed her. She had to believe that Banji was coming for her, otherwise she might as well give up now.

"...but even I knew that plan was flawed. Once the women were bought, the men had no more reason to follow Bel and he learned quickly that his influence was minimal at best. Plus, once the supply of women ran out, no one would come seeking his favor. Which brings us to now."

"Could you get on with it? Or do you plan on talking me to death?" Maria knew as soon as she said it that she shouldn't have, but she was in pain and pissed—not the best combination when you are trying to keep a cool head.

Sta'lin's face turned bright red. He looked as if he might storm out of his little observation room to put his hands on her himself. Just as suddenly as his temper flared, the calm mask he wore descended with an evil smirk.

Maria watched in horror as the cauterizing laser started up again. The metal table she was strapped on to began to heat up. Then she watched as the laser crept closer to her thigh. Instinctually she tried to pull away from it, but her ankles were held firm in their restraints. It allowed for little movement.

Maria screamed when the laser touched skin. Unlike before, where he burned her then stopped, he let the laser continue to cut and blister her flesh. Her mind reached for Banji, but she tried to hold back the connection. She didn't want him barreling in here to save her. She wanted him safe.

The Butcher giggled as he used the laser to brand Maria's flesh. She recognized the lines as Vukasin writing, but her mind was so hazed with pain that the translation device was having difficulty communicating with her brain. As best she could tell she was branded with the Vukasin word for harlot.

Suddenly the laser stopped and Maria could breathe again. She drew in shaky breaths and tried to clear her mind. This man was insane and she was caught like a fly in the spider's web.

"The Tanis royal family was wrong.… It isn't control the females and control the planet. It is control the reproduction and control the planet. I saw it long before Bel did, which is why I am his majesty's right hand man."

Sta'lin's smug look disgusted Maria. She glared at him. She had no love lost for the original ruling class, but if Sta'ling was representative of what would control this planet should the Tanis win, Maria would join the other side on principal alone. Evil like this should not be allowed to rule.

"Men want women to satisfy them and somehow they think a woman who serves only at their whim is somehow more honorable than a whore at the pleasure house, fools that they are. Fine, we will give that to them. But nothing says we have to give you to them whole." Sta'ling turned to the operating controls and began programming what he wanted the machine to do. "The well behaved women are usually sedated for this, but we both know you are anything but well behaved. Still, you are strong and your genetic material will be highly prized. We have some amazing young researchers within the Tanis clan, one of which created a way to keep biological material alive and functioning outside of the body, which makes the removal of your ovaries so much easier. Much more efficient than the embryos we created at the last lab location."

With that final declaration, Sta'ling pushed the controls to begin the procedure. A scalpel sliced open Maria's midsection. When she jerked off the table in pain, additional restraints wrapped her body until she was completely immobile. The cauterizing laser followed the scalpel to prevent her from suffering too much blood loss during the operation.

Maria lost control of the block she placed on her mind as the horrid machine dug through her internal organs. She felt the shock Banji experienced when her anguish slammed into him. She didn't blame him for locking his mind away from hers. A single tear traced down Maria's cheek; she was truly alone now.

Darkness edged against her vision as the pain overwhelmed her systems. Just as she was about to slip into blessed oblivion she felt Banji enter her mind once more. A jagged sob escaped her. He hadn't abandoned her; she wasn't alone. She reached for him and felt his love and strength surround her.

I'm sorry for retreating, jinaria, *but I had to regain control. I would never abandon you. I am coming for you. Fight, my beloved. Live for me. I need you. I will always come for you.*

The strength Banji gave her allowed Maria to push past the pain enough to realize that Sta'ling didn't want her dead yet. She fought a losing battle with the darkness. As she tumbled into unconsciousness, Maria was so glad that she had at least heard Banji's voice one last time.

CHAPTER THIRTY-TWO

Banji hoped that Korose's information was correct. He claimed that there was a military outpost in the direction Banji felt Maria when she had connected to him. Unfortunately it was nearly four days away on foot, which was why the team had piled into their transport. At a full clip they could get to the outpost in a matter of hours, but even that seemed too long.

They sped along the desert path with Daya at the controls. Allo and Boroff prepared various weapons. Eligio inventoried medical supplies, while Banji and Korose kept a look out.

"Why put an outpost in the middle of nowhere?" Banji wondered. He absently stroked Cleo's head. The shesha hadn't left his side since Maria's disappearance.

"The outpost used to be the regional slip stream station. When the Tanis closed their borders they took over all slip stream depots, supposedly to protect the populace from the enemy." Korose's tone was low and flat.

"I take it you didn't believe that piece of propaganda?"

"It just seemed to me that while they could keep others out, they also kept us in. Many would have gladly fled away from the dictates of the Tanis tyrants. There is little clan loyalty among the common folk, but the desert is an unforgiving mistress."

"And without the slip streams, you would have had to face the desert to escape."

"*Kijani*, I see something unusual up ahead," Daya interrupted their conversation.

Korose looked out into the distance and cursed.

"What is it?"

"A body."

At Banji's direction, Daya pulled up about ten yards from the body to investigate. The sun was high in the sky. It was the time of day when most of the desert retreated to find shade to wait out the intense heat. Only the buzzard raptors floated on the warm updrafts searching for carrion.

The men exited the vehicle armed and in formation. Cleo slithered ahead of them. They weren't taking chances that this might be a trap of some sort. Banji scanned the area. He directed Daya to stay with the transport and to watch their backs as the rest cautiously moved forward. They were about halfway to the body when Korose suddenly took off at a run. His bellow startled Cleo.

"Kalani!"

Banji muttered a curse but picked up the pace to follow the villager. Korose fell to his knees next to what the men were surprised to realize was the body of a woman who had been whipped until her back was shredded. Banji motioned Eligio forward, since he was trained as a field medic.

Eligio gently laid fingers against her wrist to check for a pulse. It was weak but it was there. "She's alive, Banji. Though just barely."

Korose gently turned the woman over, cradling her in his arms. Tears streaked down his cheeks and dropped on to the woman's face. Her eyes fluttered open and she reached up and touched Korose's damp face with gentle fingertips.

"You came for me."

Korose grabbed her hand and kissed her palm before laying it against his cheek.

"I will always come for you, my love."

"I'm so tired, Korose. Let me go."

"No," Korose growled. "You and me forever, Kalani. When you came back you promised me," his voice cracked, "you promised me forever."

"I'm sorry, Korose." Kalani's hand went

slack as she fell unconscious.

Eligio stood as Allo attempted to take Kalani from Korose's arms. The villager snarled at the soldier. Cleo rattled in warning, preparing to attack the villager if necessary. Banji laid a calming hand on Maria's pet.

"If you want her to live, then we need to get her back to the transport so Eligio can stabilize her," Allo spoke calmly to the distraught man.

Korose lifted Kalani as if she was the most precious treasure in the world. He walked back to the transport flanked by Allo and Boroff. Banji brought up the rear with Cleo while Eligio jogged ahead. Daya watched with cold eyes as the men entered the back of the transport. Cleo moved between the seats and out of the way. Banji stayed back.

"The Tanis have much to answer for, *kijani*." Daya nodded toward the back of the transport. "That woman needs proper medical attention. We should send her back to the village; there was a clinic there and imperial forces should be arriving soon."

"I agree, but we only have the one transport and I need its speed to get to the outpost and Maria." Banji ran a hand through his hair and sighed.

Daya whistled. "Tough choices. Which is why I have no desire to be *kijani*."

Boroff popped his head out of the back of the transport. "Allo wants to know if something is wrong since the two of you are taking so long."

Daya ruffled the younger man's hair. "Just trying to decide which woman to save this time."

"Huh?"

"The village woman needs to be taken back for proper medical treatment and Maria is still somewhere at the outpost as best we can tell, in the opposite direction."

"So do both. We are about an hour away from the outpost. Have Korose drop us off near there and then take the transport back to the village with Eligio and Kalani," Boroff said matter of factly.

"Do you have dragon-spider shit for brains? We lose our means of escape if Korose takes the transport vehicle," Daya groused.

"No, but I pay attention. Korose said the military outpost used to be the regional slip stream depot."

"What good does that do us? We are soldiers, not slip stream technicians."

"If you have coordinates of another slip stream unit, I can fire it up and get us out of there. I just can't shut it down without staying behind."

"No man gets left behind, Boroff." Banji wasn't willing to sacrifice any of his men if he could help it. "We will find another way."

"If somebody takes over driving the last hour, you will have your 'other way.'"

Banji knew if he ordered the men, they would drop behind enemy lines on a possible suicide mission in a heartbeat. But this wasn't truly a military operation. He had defied Reijo's orders to wait for reinforcements. He was simply a man trying to save the one he loved. The men followed along because they thought it was the right thing to do.

"If Eligio and Korose agree, then it looks like we are sneaking into enemy territory without a firm way out." Banji smacked Daya on the back. "I hope you are as good as you think you are."

Daya gave an evil-sounding laugh. "Leave it to me, *kijani*, this is what I do best."

"All right, you and Boroff come up with a plan. I'll take over driving until we are ready to stop."

CHAPTER THIRTY-THREE

"Please don't move, lady."

Maria slowly regained consciousness to the sound of a lilting female voice. Every part of her body hurt. She hissed out a breath as she attempted to sit up. Delicate hands pushed her shoulders, trying to get her to lie down again.

"Where am I?"

"You are in holding cell for the arena. Please, lady, your wounds haven't been entirely healed."

Maria cracked open her eyes and took stock of her body. Her tunic wasn't much more than torn rags at this point, but at least she still had her leggings and boots, though both looked worse for wear. She lifted her hand to see that it was swollen and bloodied, but it appeared that someone had wrapped it in a makeshift bandage. She looked down to see the burn on her thigh was angry and seeping; someone had been helpful enough to tear away the cloth of her leggings to keep it from sticking to the wound. Across her midsection was a large, angry-looking scar. It seemed that Sta'ling had only healed the surgical wound enough to keep her from bleeding out. Everything non-life threatening he left her to suffer with.

Maria turned to look at the woman who was helping her and was surprised to see a set of jewel-like eyes.

"You have a translator," Maria stated. "I hadn't seen any of your people with translators."

"You have seen more of my people? Here or somewhere else?"

The intensity of the woman's questions had her taken aback. But if she knew that other Earth women had been captured as well, she would want to know about it.

"I haven't personally seen any here, but I heard that they were here at least for a time. But the last time the Tanis had me I saw many of your people brought into and out of the facility I was in, but they never gave them translators." Suddenly wary of a trap, Maria asked, "How is it that you have one?"

"These *paka*," the word didn't translate but Maria could hazard a guess based on the woman's vehemence, "thought that it would be easier to direct us if a few of us could translate orders."

Maria slowly sat upright with a wince. "I'm

taking it didn't go so well."

"We could relay orders but we also finally understood what they were going to do with us. We decided that death was preferable to being slaves." Maria nodded; she definitely understood where the woman was coming from. The woman fell silent and then she tore strips of cloth from the tattered dress she wore. "We need to stop your bleeding. We are going to be thrown into the gladiator pit as prize for the victors. The experience isn't pleasant but it is survivable. But your wounds are a problem."

"I was a nurse, a healer, back on my home planet. While there are a lot of them, nothing is life threatening at the moment. My name is Maria by the way."

"Ali, I am called Ali." Ali resumed binding Maria's wounds. "We have to stop the bleeding before they put you in the pit."

"I don't understand. Why?"

"The monsters who are men...they are aggressive and angry. The cold one makes them so with drugs and pain." Maria gasped as she tightly bound a strip of cloth around the seeping burn on her thigh. "The smell of fear agitates them. The smell of blood enrages them. They tear apart anything bleeding before them, even if it is the prize they are battling to win."

Maria laid her hand over Ali's. The woman

turned pain-filled eyes to Maria. Tears shimmered in both women's eyes.

"Who was it?" Maria whispered.

"My sister…." Ali sat back on her heels and clinched her hands in her lap. "After we rebelled against the guards they decided they would use the three of us…me, my sister, and Bakra, who had been at the forefront as example to the others. They even made the native women watch as we were beaten until bloodied. They then drug us to the arena. A man they called *Khalon*—"

"Bel Tanis. He's trying to usurp the throne from the real *Khalon*. He's an evil man."

Ali snorted. "All men are evil."

"My mate is not. Neither was his brother. There are good men, and I know that they are coming for us." Maria gently touched Ali's shoulder. "Haven't you ever met at least one good man?"

Ali waved away Maria's question. "That Bel gave his soldiers a choice of one of us to be used however they wanted. The men demanded Bakra because she was the most beautiful. I do not know what happened to her when they took her away. He then told the crowd that my sister and I would be thrown into the arena with the monsters, who could have us as a prize for the night if they could keep us."

Ali wrapped her arms around her midsection

and hugged herself. Maria remained silent, not wanting to interrupt for fear that Ali would quit talking.

"Our backs were still a bloody mess from the whipping we had received. Bel picked her up by her hair and tossed her into the arena like a broken doll. The monsters were already in a frenzy, fighting each other. When my sister landed, they stopped for a moment and raised their heads like a predator scenting prey...." Tears poured down Ali's cheeks. "They fell on her and ripped her apart in their bloodlust. I can still hear her screams, but the silence that followed was even worse.... That silence weighs my heart down."

Maria scooted closer to Ali and enfolded her into her arms. The woman sobbed for the loss of her sister and the depravity she had to endure. Ali pulled away from Maria and wiped away the tears.

"That is why we have to stop your bleeding. They are putting us in the pit tonight. If we don't inflame the bloodlust, those creatures will fight to keep us from the others. I cannot keep you from having to endure a night with one of them, but in the morning the guards will come remove us and we will still be alive."

"Give me a minute." Maria closed her eyes and called out to Banji.

I am heading your way, jinaria.

How much longer? It seems we are going to be on a time crunch here.

We should be to the outpost they are holding you in within the hour. But it will take longer than that to rescue you.

Don't take too long, amore mio. They are throwing me to the wolves tonight in the gladiator arena as a prize for the victor.

Maria felt a rush of anger and possessiveness flood her mind.

They can't have you.

Just come play my knight in shining armor and save the damsel in distress.

Don't close your mind off from me. I can use our connection to help track where you are.

Banji retreated until he was just a shadow in Maria's mind. She somehow felt stronger knowing that in a way he was there with her.

CHAPTER THIRTY-FOUR

"Men, we have a bit of a situation. Maria just contacted me." Banji called over his shoulder as he increased the speed of the transport vehicle. He was relieved to hear from her despite the news she imparted.

"So she is alive?" Boroff asked. Daya punched the young man in the shoulder and rolled his eyes.

"Yes, but I don't think they treated her fully from the torture I felt earlier. I could still feel pain through our connection, though it was much more manageable. That isn't our biggest complication though."

Banji swerved to miss an out cropping of rock. The sudden jerk of the vehicle caused Kalani to moan, alerting everyone that she was awake. Banji glanced behind before turning back to the front. Between Korose and Eligio, the woman had been stabilized, but she still needed medical attention.

Banji continued. "According to Maria, they are taking her to a gladiatorial match to be a prize for the winner."

Kalani sat up, gasping in pain. She grabbed Korose's arm and begged. "You have to save her; she will die."

Korose tried to soothe Kalani but she just became more agitated.

Kalani sobbed. "You don't understand.... Those fighters aren't men anymore. They have been turned into some kind of monster. They will kill her."

"Well, dragon spider shit." Daya went back to furiously working on his surprises for their attack.

As the transport neared the outpost, the walls of a stone valley began to rise around them. Korose directed them to a little-known side valley that Banji would have missed if it hadn't been pointed out to him.

The men climbed out of the transport vehicle and started arming themselves. While all carried the bladed hand-to-hand weapons considered more honorable by most Vukasins, they also packed various guns. Experience had taught them that most of the Tanis didn't believe in the ideal of looking a man in the eyes if you had to kill them.

Daya had various different canisters strapped

to his body. Allo had told Banji that Daya was an explosives expert, and tonight they were going to put his skills to use. Banji just wished that they had had time so he could have assessed Daya's skills first hand. But he trusted his friend and they were short on time, so Allo's word was going to have to be good enough.

"I know I can't phase, but I can fight if you need me."

Banji looked the older man over. It was true that they could use some more manpower, but Korose, while strong, wasn't a trained soldier. Banji also knew that they would have to fight the deformed phased. Without a phased state of his own, Korose would be walking into his death.

"I appreciate the offer, but we both know that Kalani needs more medical attention than a field medic could give her. You've got to get her back to the village clinic."

"You think I would be a liability because I am not a warrior."

That was exactly what Banji thought, but he wasn't going to say so. Korose was an honorable man and had his pride.

"The women are our priority, and that includes Kalani. Besides, imperial soldiers should be arriving soon. I need you to give them coordinates to this place as well as the valley prison. They will most likely need your expertise in scouting the area as well." Banji sighed. "I'm also sending Eligio back with you. That, more than anything, should tell you why I am sending you back."

Korose looked to the twilight sky, watching the moons overhead. "You know Kalani is my mate. I've known that since we were both children. I should have bonded us and taken her away, no matter what the law said. I might have been able to spare her the horrors she experienced if I had."

Banji's heart ached to hear the guilt in Korose's voice—so many lives hurt by a government that tried to regulate private lives out of fear.

"There is no law stopping you now. She is going to need your love more than ever. You can't change the past, but you can help the future move forward." Banji held out his hand to Korose, who hesitated a second before grasping his forearm in the age-old warriors embrace. Banji pulled a pulse rifle out of the back of the transport and handed it to Korose before stepping away. "Take your woman; keep her safe."

Korose shouldered the rifle and nodded before turning back to the transport. Banji watched as they drove off out of sight. The four men climbed to the top of the valley wall while Cleo paced back and forth below. Each surveyed the military facility through his battle helmet. Banji adjusted his metal battle collar; he knew before the battle was over he would have to phase and he needed to plan for the weakness that entailed.

Once Banji saw a pattern to the Tanis patrols, he reached for Maria over their bond. It didn't take him long to find her presence in a building next to the large open air arena. Unfortunately, that was on the other side of the outpost from their way out. Getting to the slip stream facility was going to be tricky.

"Alright, men; it's time to go hunting."

CHAPTER THIRTY-FIVE

Maria stood up and started to examine the room they were in. It was slow going because she was still in a lot of pain from Sta'lin's little operation. Like the medical facility and holding cells, this room was completely manmade. She smoothed her hands over the surface of the walls and metal supports.

"What are you doing?" Ali stood and came next to Maria.

"I'm looking for any weaknesses, but I am also looking for surveillance devices."

Maria found what she was looking for in the far corner. A tiny crystal camera was in place of one of the metal rivets on the support beam. She never would have noticed it if she hadn't been looking for it.

I can feel you close, Banji. You need to know they have surveillance here like they did at the prison.

I'll keep that in mind. We have a lock on your location, but getting to the extraction point is going to be a challenge.

There is another woman in the cell with me. I don't know how many others are here. There was another who tried to escape with me, but they took her away.

We found a badly beaten woman in the desert named Kalani.

That's her!

She needed medical attention so we sent her back to the village.

Maria sighed with relief. She hadn't realized how worried she had been about Kalani's fate until that moment.

Maria, you and the other woman have to be ready. Keep your wits about you. Trust no one but Allo, Boroff, Daya, or myself.

Just hurry up and get us out of here.

I love you.

Maria hesitated. She hadn't expected Banji to declare his love. Did she love him back? She thought she had loved Gio, but her feelings for Banji were so much stronger; but their time together was so much shorter. Could love come this soon?

You don't have to say anything, Maria. I just wanted you to know, just in case....

Just in case they died tonight. Banji closed off their connection and Maria felt bereft. If Maria had learned anything in this whole mess it was that tomorrow was never promised. She could let her fears and doubts hold her back, but what if she missed something truly wonderful just because she worried it might not last?

"Are you all right?" Ali laid a delicate hand on Maria's arm.

Maria realized she was crying. That right there told her that time didn't matter; she loved Banji. Now all she wanted to do was crash into his mind and tell him that she loved him back. If it hadn't been for the fact that she knew he was infiltrating enemy territory and distracting him could get them all killed, she would have. She would just have to make sure they both survived so she could tell him to his face.

Maria wrapped her arms around Ali and sobbed loudly. In between her noisy cries of, "I want to go home," Maria whispered into Ali's ear, "A rescue party knows where we are. They are coming for us tonight; be ready."

Ali patted Maria's back and played along. That was how the guards found them.

"Let's go. Sta'ling and his customers are waiting." One of the guards, a man with hard eyes, zapped Maria out of Ali's arms with a device similar to a cattle prod.

"Ow." Maria rubbed her thigh and glared at the guard, who just grinned at her evilly.

"Make sure you give them a good show tonight, female. Make enough money for the bosses and they might let you live until tomorrow." He laughed at his own poor joke. None of the other guards joined him.

Maria didn't dignify him with a response. She stood tall and concentrated on not letting her pain show. She grabbed Ali's hand and the pair preceded the guards out of the cell door.

Logically, Maria knew that they hadn't traveled far, but the trek had been uphill and her abused body was screaming that it had had enough. She shoved the pain away and locked it behind a door in her mind. It was a trick she had learned to push past exhaustion when she had to work a straight twenty-four hours in the trauma center: lock away what is in the way; concentrate on the task at hand.

The guards took them to an area at the bottom of the arena that was built into the ground. There was a reason people called this place "The Pit." They passed dozens of cages filled with the deformed phased. Guards were everywhere. They shoved Maria and Ali into a small holding area that had a gate that opened into the arena.

It was much larger than she had expected. It

reminded her somewhat of the stadium when Italy had hosted the World Cup of Soccer. Her *nonno* was an avid soccer fan and had taken her to the game that year. There seemed to be just as many people packed into the stands. But unlike a soccer match, the people here were waiting to watch men kill each other.

Maria chanced contacting Banji. He needed to know what he was walking into. It was in the back of her mind to warn him off so she could know he would live.

Life wouldn't be worth living without you, jinaria. *I'm coming for you.*

Please, be careful, Banji.

Always....

CHAPTER THIRTY-SIX

"You are insane!"

Banji knew that Allo would have issues with the plan, but they didn't have time to argue about it. They had snuck into one of the buildings near the arena after night had fallen. It appeared to be filled with offices, most likely for the Tanis military officers. Getting in had been surprisingly simple. The vast majority of the personnel were gathered at the gladiatorial event. Those few left behind were grumbling and inattentive because they had been assigned guard duty.

The four men slipped into a posh office, and the young soldier, Boroff, showed off his technical prowess by hacking into their computer system. It gave Banji hope that the whelp would actually be able to operate the slip stream to get them out of here.

Boroff had called up the specs for the entire

outpost. They were using the detailed map to plan their mission.

Banji pointed to the slip stream depot. "Boroff, you and Allo will head here and prepare the slip stream. We will have the Tanis on our heels and will need to slip on the run." He turned to Daya. "Are you sure that Allo can handle the placement of our parting gift?"

"As long as he doesn't start the countdown, we are good."

Banji nodded then enlarged the arena area on the map. "I'll infiltrate here and find the women…"

"*Kijani*, we have a problem." Boroff was navigating through a series of screens on the holo-feed. "According to this cargo manifest, there are about forty females being housed in this building here," Boroff pointed to a large structure near the slip stream depot. "If I'm reading this right, they are to be shipped out to auction tomorrow."

"Auction? You mean these bastards are selling the women?" Daya growled.

"Boroff, copy that information and see if you can find their destination coordinates. Reijo is going to want that information," Banji directed.

"We can't just leave them," Allo growled at Banji. "If they auction them off they will be scattered to all corners of the universe and we will never find them again."

"I hadn't planned on leaving them. Maria would never forgive me if I left the women behind again to save her." Banji's eyes turned flat and cold. "There can be no mistakes in this operation. You are going to kill silently to pull this off. That means up close and personal. If you don't think you can handle that, I need to know now."

All three men stared back at Banji, waiting for him to continue. They would get those women to freedom or die trying.

"If we are lucky, all the facilities are on skeleton crews as the majority of the soldiers attend the fight. We will have to take out the patrols at the slip stream depot first without setting off any alarms. Once that is accomplished, Allo, you will be responsible for getting the women out and to the stream. Daya can cover you for a short time, but I will need him to get Maria out. Do you have the coordinates I gave you?"

Boroff nodded. All three men turned to the door when they heard a quiet scuffle on the other side. Banji signaled for the other men to be quiet as he cracked open the door. On the other side he found Cleo silently squeezing the life out of one of the Tanis guards. Banji quickly pulled Cleo and the body of the guard into the office.

"Damn, I guess that is our cue to get moving. Boroff, use this authorization code to get a message to Kavi." Banji programmed a code into a crystal communicator and handed it to the young soldier. He then stripped the dead Tanis guard and traded out his own clothing for the Tanis uniform while he continued with his instructions. "He should be able to get a message to Reijo and Ghaleb. You have all got your assignments?" He looked around the room at his small band of men. If they pulled off this rescue it was going to be a small miracle. "Right, I'm heading in to the arena."

"May you stand while your enemy falls," Allo intoned the ancient warrior farewell and saluted Banji. Banji slipped into the night with Cleo silently slithering beside him.

*****

Maria watched out of the bars of her holding cell as the arena filled to capacity. It seemed that almost every soldier in the place was there tonight. But it wasn't just soldiers settling in to watch the carnage. To the right was a series of platforms that were lavishly decorated. The men sitting in those areas were expensively dressed and quietly sipped drinks served by scantily clad females from numerous different species. A hologram flying high above the center of the arena gave up-to-date odds for a myriad of different gambling bets.

As best as Maria could tell there was going to be half a dozen different matches, including at least one melee battle. Those that survived would get the chance to battle for her and Ali as a prize. She swallowed when she saw that they were giving odds of her survival as three to one.

She turned away from the view of the arena. She could feel Banji nearby and she prayed that they would be able to all get out of this place alive tonight. Banji had told her about the dozens of women that they located in another building. He had asked her to forgive him for taking longer to get to her so his team could get those women out. She would be lying if she said that she hadn't had selfish thoughts of wanting him to come and get her first, but she would never have been able to live with herself if she left another group of women behind. Besides, they had a little bit of time. The preliminary fights had to finish up before the main event could take place.

Ali was curled up in the corner trying to get what rest she could. Maria knew she should probably do the same, but she was too keyed up to sleep, so she paced instead.

The roar of the crowd had increased so much that Maria almost missed the sound of the lock disengaging. Standing in the doorway was Krac. He looked even worse than he did when she paralyzed him. Fur shimmered over his body and he was clenching his jaw to keep it from contorting. His eyes shimmered with excitement.

"You're mine, you little whore," he growled around his shifting teeth. "I've been given permission to participate in the main event, and when I win, I will make you suffer for the humiliation you have caused me."

Maria just stood staring Krac down. She knew that if he got his hands on her she would not live to see tomorrow. The thought terrified her, but she wasn't about to let him see that.

Another guard pulled Krac away from their cell. Krac turned and snarled at the man but eventually left. The door was closed and the locks set once again. Maria sank to the floor, grateful for the first time to be separated by a cell door with the rest of the compound. Krac was going to be a problem. Sta'ling had obviously experimented on him, but he hadn't been completely reduced to a creature acting only on instinct. He was losing control but for now still had the ability to think and strategize. That would give him the edge when the main event started. Maria's prayed that Banji was able to get her out before then.

CHAPTER THIRTY-SEVEN

Banji kept his head down and shuffled behind a group of Tanis guards heading into the arena. Cleo seemed to understand the need to stay out of sight and silent. The only reason Banji spotted her in the shadows was because he already knew that she was there.

It was surprisingly easy to slip into the building. Everyone simply saw his uniform and let him pass without a second look. Discipline seemed almost non existent here. No, looking further it wasn't a lack of discipline because he saw soldiers carefully caring for their weapons. It was apathy. These men had no real loyalty to those who ruled over them; they simply did the job out of fear or for money.

Recalling the map of the arena that Banji had memorized, he made his way to the lower levels where the fighters were housed in cages. Maria had said that her holding cell opened onto the arena floor, so she had to be on the lower level.

Banji discovered a vast warren of cells and cages. It would take forever to find Maria if he had to search each and every one. He then remembered Cleo had tracked Maria for a while back in the village.

He checked to see that the hallway he was in was clear.

"Cleo," he whispered. "Come on, girl. I need you."

A shadow shifted in the corner and Banji saw the large shesha move towards him.

Banji crouched down and stroked the serpent's head. He wasn't sure if this was going to work, but it was worth a try.

"Alright, Cleo. Find Maria." Cleo cocked her head to the side and flicked her forked tongue at Banji. "Find her."

Banji was about to give up when Cleo turned and scented the air with her tongue. She weaved her head back and forth until she seemed to zone-in on something. Without a sound, the shesha took off at such a pace that Banji had trouble keeping up with her. He hoped that if anyone spotted them they would just think that he was trying to capture Cleo to get rid of her.

*****

Ali woke up when Sta'ling appeared on the

270

hologram above the area. He thanked the patrons and introduced the first round of fights. Maria stood next to Ali and observed what was going on through the bars of their holding area. Six separate cages had been erected on the arena floor. Chained beside each of the cages was a pair of the deformed phased. There were multiple guards surrounding the creatures.

The guards used the cattle prod type devices to keep the snarling creatures apart. Already in their maddened state, they were lashing out at anything that came near them. It had many of the guards phasing to help control them.

"By the stars, they are worse than last time," Ali gasped, turning pale. She backed away from the bars, her hand covering her mouth. "We won't survive if they get a hold of us."

"It will be all right, Ali. Have faith."

Maria turned back to the arena. She strained to see the faces of the people in the stands. Banji was somewhere nearby; she could feel him. She figured that he probably snuck in with the crowds. She was hoping to catch a glimpse of his face or Allo, Daya...hell, at this point she would even take the young soldier Boroff.

Maria screamed when warm blood splattered across her face from the nearest cage. She had been so intent on finding her rescuers that she hadn't paid attention to the matches that had started.

She turned to see where the blood had come from and wished she hadn't. The victorious deformed phased had ripped the arm off of his opponent and was currently beating him to death with it.

Maria had seen severed limbs before, but the brutality of the attack coupled with the dying creature's painful whimpers and cries turned her stomach. The crowd's cheer at the blood sport made her sick. Maria backed away from the gate to the arena and tried to wipe the blood from her face. She had no way of blocking out the sound of the carnage, but she didn't have to watch it. The roar of the crowd and the pained death cries of the creatures forced to fight blurred together until it was just a cacophony of sound punctuated by the occasional announcement.

Maria was beginning to worry; as best she could tell they were in the final set of elimination rounds before the main event, and she still hadn't heard from Banji. What if he had been captured? Or injured? What if they couldn't make it past the security in the area? What if…?

"You really do think too much, *jinaria.*"

Banji's beloved voice carried from the window of the holding cell door. Maria jumped up and reached through the small opening in the door. She had to touch him to make sure that he was really there. Banji entwined his fingers with hers, briefly. Cleo pushed her way between their hands, demanding Maria's attention with a frantic rattle.

"Hush, you scaly beast. Do you want them to catch us?"

Ali came to the door during Maria's reunion.

"You!" Maria turned at Ali's outburst. She obviously recognized Banji, but that wasn't possible. "How did you escape? I heard that they were sending you off world."

Banji rubbed the back of his neck. "I think you are mistaking me for my brother."

"No, I know your face. I don't think Maria would be jealous just because you saved me."

Maria touched Ali's arm. She didn't know anything about Ali's world. It is possible that identical twins was a concept that she wasn't familiar with.

"He's not lying to you. Banji has been with me the entire time. His twin brother, who looks just like him, allowed himself to be captured so we could escape the Tanis prison."

Cleo's rattle appeared in the opening of the door. The comical sight of the shesha trying to get into the cell broke the growing tension. Banji surveyed the cell and noticed that the bars leading to the arena floor might allow Cleo to squeeze though. He would feel better if the women had the protection of the venomous serpent.

Banji addressed Ali. "M'lady, I need you to tell Maria everything you know about my brother, please."

"*Dio*, Banji! We are being monitored!" Maria hung her head in her hands. "*Stupido.*"

Banji whistled, and when Maria looked up she saw him waving some sort of crystal device. "I'm fairly certain all non-essential personnel are at the arena, but just in case, I brought along this signal disrupter. As long as I am here all they will get is static, which is why I have to hurry."

"You have to get us out of here before the main event, Banji. One of the combatants really wants to hurt me, and I don't think he will wait until he wins to try."

"*Frex!*" Banji pulled at his hair. "We've got to hold off for a bit longer; getting the other women to the extraction point is taking longer than expected." He tried to reach Maria through the small opening in the cell door but couldn't. She moved so he could give her face a gentle caress. "I'm going to try and send Cleo in to you. She can protect you if I can't get you out before the main event starts. If I have to I will phase and join the chaos of the match to get to you. Keep the other woman near you; don't let them split you up. Alright?"

Maria nodded and stepped away from the

door. "Go, before you are discovered."

With a last longing look, Banji was gone.

CHAPTER THIRTY-EIGHT

Maria sat against the cell wall and patted the space next to her for Ali to sit. "Tell me about the man who saved you."

"He was among the creatures…men, who had been in the pit the day that my sister died. They had him chained and were hitting him repeatedly with those painful stick things. I think they were trying to force him into becoming one of those monsters." Ali's unfocused eyes looked into the past. "When the one called Bel threw my sister into the pit, it was then that the man changed into a beast and broke his chains, but it was too late to save my sister."

Ali's account was interrupted when a tell-tale rattle was heard by the arena gate. The woman's eyes got huge and she tried to clamor up the wall.

"What is that?"

The giant serpent curled around as Maria giggled. It raised up and Maria could see that Ali was afraid she was about to be eaten.

"It's all right. This is Cleo, she's actually very gentle with me, but be careful of her fangs, she is venomous."

Ali slowly sat back down. She flinched when Cleo got in her face and flicked her forked tongue at her. Cleo decided that Ali was alright and curled herself around both women. Ali stroked a hand down the creature's body. Its scales were surprisingly warm and silky.

"Aren't you worried that they are going to see Cleo?"

Maria shrugged. "It doesn't matter, they wouldn't dare enter the cell with a fully grown wild shesha. And if they were stupid enough to try, Cleo would probably kill them. Back to Akia…."

"Akia?"

"Banji's brother, the one who saved you."

Ali absently petted Cleo. "I never knew his name. He pulled me out of the mass of monsters and acted as my shield. Even when he changed, it was obvious that he was more in control of himself than the others, though I think it was a battle to stay in control."

"Why do you say that?"

"Just a feeling I suppose." Ali turned her head and looked at Maria. "When the others finally quit attacking him, he told me not to fear him—that he didn't desire me but another. When I saw Banji, I thought you might have been his other."

Maria shook her head, "We haven't seen Akia since the day we escaped. I didn't actually get to interact with him much since I was unconscious for much of the escape."

"They ripped me away from Akia and gave me to another. I heard Bel declare that he was wasted talent here and that he was taking him away. Sta'ling was not happy. He raged for days at the loss of Akia. Rumor had it Sta'ling thought that he had achieved some kind of breakthrough in his experiments with Akia."

"I don't suppose you know where they took Akia to?"

Ali shrugged. "No, I don't, but I don't think it is on this planet."

"What makes you say that?"

"These *pakas* have subjugated my people and created their own kingdom on my planet. Here they are at war; on my home world they are not. What is to say that they haven't done this on other worlds?"

Maria was thoughtful. She wondered if Banji's people had any idea how big the scope of the Tanis problem really was. She was about to say something more when the lock disengaged and the door swung open.

Cleo raised up, hood unfurled and fangs

dripping.

"What the *frex!*" The guard stumbled back, not expecting to be faced with a wild shesha. "Where in the five hells did that come from?"

"What's taking so long?" Another guard came up behind the first. When he saw the angry shesha he slammed the door closed.

"What the hell are we supposed to do now? Sta'ling wants them on the arena floor."

"Did you see the fangs on that thing? They were dripping with venom. That's no lost pet."

He double checked the holding cell through the little window. Cleo snapped at the guard, causing him to fall on his ass. He got up and glared at the door. Maria had to stifle a giggle because she was fairly certain he had just pissed himself.

"This holding cell has a gate to the arena floor. Call Jax in the control room and tell him to open it up and use the sweeper to push them out. Sta'ling wanted them out there; he didn't specify how."

"What about the shesha?"

"Are you going to go in there and get it out?" When the other guard didn't respond, he sneered, "I didn't think so. If it kills off some of the experiments, better them than us."

With that last callous comment, the guards walked away from the cell.

Maria and Ali waited for what would happen next in quiet anticipation. It didn't take long for the gate to the arena to rise up. When the women didn't move from the safety of the holding cell, a mechanical whine started up.

Maria and Ali looked around, trying to see where the noise was coming from. Then the wall at the back of the cell hit their backs. It moved ponderously slow, but each slow inch moved them toward the arena floor and there was nothing the women could do about it. Even Cleo hissed her displeasure about being pushed out.

Banji, where are you? They are pushing us out into the arena.

I'm making my way to the arena now. I just met up with Daya. The women are at the slip stream and Boroff has started sending them through.

That's all well and good, but what about Ali and I?

I'm not leaving without you. I don't have time to explain, just be ready no matter what happens. I love you.

I love you too.

The bright lights of the arena blinded Maria for a moment. She raised her hand to shield them until they could adjust. Cat calls and whistles in a multitude of languages echoed through the space. Maria was shocked to see more than just Vukasins in the stands, now that she had a clear view of them.

Banji had made the conflict sound like it was an internal planetary issue. He and Akia had seemed shocked that Ali's people were being brought to Vukas. But from what she was seeing, the Tanis had spread their slimy fingers into many other worlds. This could be very bad for Banji and the empire.

"Gentlemen, it would seem that our prizes have found a way to arm themselves," a loud voice boomed over the arena. "In light of the new player, please give us a moment to recalculate the odds. Shesha serpents are highly venomous and can be vicious when guarding their nest. How many challengers do you think it will take out before being killed?"

The crowd shouted out numbers and demanded to place new bets. Maria laid a hand on Cleo's hood as the shesha became more agitated. Cleo leaned into Maria's touch, seeking reassurance, but she didn't put down her hood.

"Bets are now closed.... Bets are now closed."

The crowd roared and grumbled. Maria straightened her spine after she heard a particularly lewd comment thrown at her and Ali. Inside she trembled in fear, but she would be damned before she let these bastards see her fear.

"Eyes and ears open, Ali. We will have to

move at a moment's notice."

Ali didn't say anything and Maria worried that perhaps fear had overwhelmed her. But when she looked over at Ali, the woman was staring intently at the raised dais at one side of the arena. Her face looked murderous.

Maria focused where Ali was staring. She could just barely make out Sta'lin's thin frame standing next to an extravagantly dressed man. Judging by the rage on Ali's face, this must be Bel. Only the man who murdered her sister would deserve such a reaction. Maria laid a hand on Ali's shoulder and gave a squeeze.

"Gentlemen, if you would direct your attention to the far side of the arena!"

Maria's eyes followed the crowds. Behind three different gates, similar to the one she and Ali had been pushed out of, were a half dozen of the deformed phased. Already they snarled and tore at each other within their holding cells.

Damsel in distress, paging knight in shining armor.

I'm here. Don't be afraid.

A little too late for that.

"We have a treat for you tonight, gentleman! Our regular games will be more vicious, more bloody. Tonight our animals don't just fight for survival, they fight for the prize all males want: the chance to have their way with one of two females...or both at the same time if their prowess proves able."

The crowd hooted and jeered at the licentious comment. The idea of one of those violent monsters putting his hands on her made Maria's skin crawl. Cleo felt her master's distress and paced back and forth between the women with a serpentine slither, stopping every so often to hiss towards the other end of the arena.

"Let the games begin!" shouted the announcer.

Everything stopped, pausing in anticipation. The groan of the holding cell gates opening echoed through the space. Then all hell broke loose.

The deformed phased spilled out of the holding cells, most battling each other, oblivious to the women at the other end of the arena—all except one.

The largest monster was wearing a Tanis guard uniform and a battle collar, where all of the others seemed to be naked from the waist up. This creature searched for the women. When he spotted Maria, he spread his arms wide and bellowed in rage. The other creatures cringed and their eyes darted around, looking for the danger. When they decided that they weren't the focus of the behemoth's rage, they went back to killing each other.

"Krac," Maria whispered as that thing charged them. *Dio,* he was going to kill her and she couldn't stop him.

Maria shoved Ali behind her. She was useless as a protector, but at least she might be able to buy the other woman some time. Where the hell was Banji?

Cleo reared up to strike at Krac, when she was suddenly knocked out of the way by a streak of fur in a Tanis uniform coming from behind them. The new player attacked Krac with a ferocity Maria had never seen before.

Both men ripped and tore at each other with fang and claw. They were a blur of grunts and growls. It was difficult to see where one ended and the other began. Maria saw that the one battling Krac also wore a battle collar around his neck. That meant neither one of the pair could paralyze the other and end this quickly. It became a battle of strategy and stamina.

Maria heard Ali scream. She whipped around to find the other woman being drug off by one of the deformed. She had been so engrossed in the epic battle before her she forgot to watch for the others.

"Cleo!" Maria called and gestured towards Ali. Thankfully the shesha seemed to understand what Maria wanted and took off after Ali and her attacker. Cleo sank her fangs into the deformed's leg. The creature howled in pain and released Ali to face the new threat. Unfortunately for the creature, a shesha's venom is fast acting. It was only a matter of minutes before the deformed phase's attacks devolved into seizures. Cleo wrapped her large body around the collapsed creature, squeezing the life out of him until glassy eyes and a foam-filled mouth were all that remained.

Maria grabbed Ali and the pair ran along the edge of the arena, searching for cover. Unfortunately, the space was wide open; even the holding cells offered no refuge as the walls had been pushed to the front like their cell had, probably to move the creatures out into the open. That left the women with no place to retreat to.

The only choice was too keep running, but Maria's body wasn't going to be able to do that for long. Already her midsection hurt and her limbs felt like lead. It was probably one of the reasons Sta'ling hadn't healed all of her wounds.

Maria skidded to a stop and attempted to change directions when a deformed suddenly appeared in front of her. He reached out to grab her with his clawed hands, but she avoided his grasp. His claws raked across her upper arm, leaving bloody gouges.

Ali looked at her in horror as Maria grabbed her arm to staunch the flow of blood. The remaining deformed froze, raising their snouts to the air. Collectively they scented the air and sent an eerie howl to the heavens.

Maria remembered what Ali had said about the deformed phased going into a deadly bloodlust. Their eyes zeroed in on Maria and her heart stopped.

"GO!" Maria shoved Ali away from her. She didn't want the woman caught up in the danger she saw in the deformeds' eyes.

CHAPTER THIRTY-NINE

Banji had hoped to watch over Maria from the shadows until Daya confirmed they were ready for phase two of their plan. His intentions went out the window when the largest of the gladiators zeroed in and charged the women. Banji couldn't let that thing get his claws on the woman he loved.

He shifted into his phased form and rushed out onto the arena floor. He hit the attacker like a speeding transport, but the man barely budged. Whatever Sta'ling was pumping into their systems made them abnormally strong.

"I can smell her stink all over you. The whore is mine!" the creature snarled.

Banji snapped his jaws at the phased's face as he raked exposed flesh with his claws. He went for the throat, hoping to end this quickly, but his claws connected with metal. So this one wore a battle collar, unlike the others. That information, coupled with what Maria had told him, let him know that this was most likely the sadistic guard Krac that had brutalized and terrorized Maria in the valley prison and here.

"Krac," Banji growled as they grappled.

Krac smirked. "I see my reputation precedes me."

If he had just been another victim of experiments, Banji might have just incapacitated him. But he had just signed his death warrant with his smirk. Banji punched the man in the solar plexus, robbing him of breath. He jumped away to put some space between them.

While Krac was still recovering from the blow to his chest, Banji swept his legs out from under him, putting him on the ground. Banji chanced a look around trying to spot Maria. He found her cornered by three of the deformed. They only thing keeping them at bay was the angry shesha between them and Maria.

He needed to finish off Krac quickly. Banji reared back and kicked Krac in the head as the creature rolled over and tried to push himself off the ground. The blow dazed him enough that he momentarily shifted out of his phased state. With his concentration compromised, Krac seemed to have difficulty maintaining control.

If time wasn't of the essence, Banji might have been more interested in what that might mean, but all of his thoughts were on the safety of his mate. Banji jumped on Krac's back and wrapped his clawed hands around the monster's throat.

Krac bucked and clawed, trying to dislodge Banji. The battle collar prevented Banji from applying enough pressure to crush Krac's airway, and the slow suffocation just wasn't fast enough. Banji used the leverage his hands afforded to start bashing Krac's head against the battle-hardened ground.

A few sharp blows to Krac's unprotected head and the man was unconscious and unphased. His human form was much more vulnerable to injury. Banji couldn't afford to risk Krac coming after Maria again, so he made short work of the man. He continued to bash his head against the ground. It was vicious, brutal, messy work. A sickening crunch and Krac no longer breathed.

As soon as that threat was neutralized, Banji jumped up and roared a challenge to the remaining deformed.

"What a show, gentlemen…what a show!" the announcer boomed across the arena; reminding Banji that these selfish bastards were watching the carnage as entertainment. "What an upset. Our champion has been defeated and we are down to our final few combatants. Who will be crowned the new champion? Will it be the upstart new comer? Keep your eye on the floor and remember tonight's special on our vintage wydam wine."

Banji ran towards Maria as she moved behind the protection of Cleo. One body lay at Maria's feet, twitching with the last of its convulsions, a victim of the shesha's deadly bite. Two of the deformed circled just out of reach of the beast, hoping to find an opening to snatch the bleeding Maria. Ali was nowhere in sight. Banji rushed the remaining deformed, quickly paralyzing them with swift blows to the side of the neck.

Unlike Krac, these were mindless monsters working strictly on instinct. Sta'ling probably left their battle collars off on purpose so he would have an easy "kill switch" if they got out of hand. Cleo quickly bit the helpless creatures, insuring they would never rise again. Protecting Maria was evidently hungry work because Cleo wrapped the smallest deformed phased in her coils and promptly proceeded to swallow him.

Banji rush to Maria, who screamed and thrashed when he grabbed her. If Cleo hadn't been occupied, Banji probably would have gotten bitten.

"Be calm, *jinaria*." Banji's voice was distorted around his canine-like snout and teeth. "It's me."

Maria stared intently at the creature before her. She had never seen Banji phase, so she had no idea what he looked like. Her gaze locked in on his eyes as if she was trying to see the soul of the man within. After a moment, her hard eyes softened as she reached up to touch his cheek near his eyes.

"Banji..." she sighed with a questioning breath.

Banji unphased and wrapped Maria in his arms. He murmured into her hair his fear for her and his joy that she was safe. Banji forgot for a moment that they weren't safe yet.

"No it's not possible.... That man is caged on Ludus Prime," Banji heard a voice from the dais above them.

"I told you that two of them attempted the escape from the Moon Valley facility and we were only able to recover on of them," Sta'ling calmly informed the man standing next to him.

Banji recognized the pompously dressed man as Bel Tanis, the false *Khalon*.

"Guards! Seize the Tiaret spy!" Bel bellowed.

"Any day now, Daya," Banji grumbled as dozens of guards spilled into the arena.

Just then an explosion rocked the building. Everyone froze for a moment before pandemonium erupted. Patrons stampeded over each other, trying to get out as a series of other explosions occurred in different areas of the arena complex. The guards looked around, unsure what to do as Sta'ling and Bel shouted contradictory orders at them.

Banji had been counting off the number of explosions under his breath. He suddenly covered Maria's body with his own. "Take cover."

He phased as one final explosion blew a hole in the side of the arena. Maria could hear Banji grunting as debris pelted his back. He shielded her with his own body. When they looked up, most of the guards were dead or injured. As the dust settled, Daya sauntered in with a smirk on his face and a woman slung over his shoulder.

"I think you lost something." Daya sat Ali on her feet in front of Maria. Maria wrapped the woman in a hug as Daya said, "See, I told you I was one of the good guys."

*****

"Hate to break up this love fest, ladies, but we need to get out of here." Daya started to physically push Ali as she glared at him. He directed them towards the gaping hole in the side of the building.

Maria was exhausted and in pain, but they hadn't escaped yet. She dug deep and found a reserve of energy fueled by survival. It was difficult with her wounds, but she managed to keep up with the group as they wove in and out of the shadows.

The streets of the compound were eerily silent. The only noise came from the people trying to escape the arena. Maria knew there should be other personnel around.

"Where is everyone?" Maria whispered to Banji.

"I don't know...." Banji surveyed the area. Sta'ling should have sounded an alarm and had this place swarming with reserve soldiers.

Daya chuckled. "You didn't think that the only thing I was good for was blowing stuff up, did you?"

The group rounded a corner and nearly tripped over a Tanis soldier snoring in a corner. Daya nudged the man with his boot to the protest of everyone else. The soldier snorted loudly and just rolled over without waking.

"Big booms aren't the only kind of bomb I can make. I gassed the entire route back to the slip stream depot. I doubt I got everyone, but I got enough to buy us the time we need to get out of here, hopefully."

The team moved quickly through the quiet streets. Banji and Daya grabbed weapons from various sleeping soldiers along the way. Maria was thankful for their foresight, as personnel started to stir the closer they got to the slip stream.

The group was so intent on getting to their destination as quickly as possible that Banji turned, ready to defend himself, when Maria grabbed his arm to stop him. She was staring up at the building that housed the medical facility.

"What's wrong?" Banji asked.

"I can't leave yet, Banji. There is something I have to do first."

Maria turned and looked at Banji, and the look in her eyes froze his soul. She knew the delaying would almost eliminate her chance to escape, but whatever she felt she had to do was worth her gambling her life.

Banji called Daya over. "You get the woman to the slip stream. Delay leaving as long as you can, but if it comes to it, leave us behind."

Daya started to protest and Banji gave him the *kijani* glare. Daya huffed but nodded. He would follow orders even if he didn't want to. He grabbed Ali, who squirmed to be let go. She didn't trust a Vukasin male alone. She felt safer with Maria. Finally, Daya threw her over his shoulder and took off at a run.

"You should go with them, Banji."

Banji cupped Maria's cheek and used his thumb to wipe away a stray tear that escaped from her eyes.

"I go where you go, *jinaria*." He gazed into her eyes, willing her to understand that he needed her in his life. "Now tell me what in that building has you so upset. But tell me on the move."

CHAPTER FORTY

Cleo herded Maria from the rear as she ran next to Banji. Maria huffed and puffed as she told Banji what Sta'ling had done to her. The more he heard, the more determined Banji was to kill Sta'ling Tanis. When she got to the part where Sta'ling had sterilized her and stolen her ovaries to create babies as a future commodity. Banji understood why she had to take care of this before she could escape. It would have haunted her if she thought there was even a chance that her children might end up being bought and sold like livestock.

So together they made their way through the medical facility. Banji slowed the pace once they were inside. Numerous doors and intersecting hallways made this building a warren of possible ambush sites.

Banji lifted a finger to his lips, signaling Maria to keep quiet. Around the next corner he could hear voices.

"I don't care if they are still unconscious; leave them behind. Load up the inventory and get to the transports."

Banji saw two men in Tanis uniforms salute and turn on their heel to fulfill orders. Banji was more interested in the two remaining men, Bel and Sta'ling Tanis. Somehow they had made it from the arena to the medical facility well ahead of them. That shouldn't have been possible, as their group had taken the most direct route.

Banji and Maria followed the pair at a discreet distance. If there were hidden passages connecting the buildings, they needed to know because that could spell disaster for the women waiting to be slip streamed out.

"We knew we would have to abandon the border posts sooner or later. All this does is move up the time frame for us," Bel said to Sta'ling.

"I have invaluable research data both here and in the valley prison facility. I can't just abandon it."

"Forget about your twice-damned research; reports have a Tiaret unit attacking the prison facility. It is only a matter of time before it falls. The attack here may be guerilla warfare instead of a military offensive, but you know just as well as I do that this facility is compromised. While I admit your experiments have been profitable, it's not like you can't recreate them in another facility."

"You don't understand," Sta'ling practically whined.

"Enough," Bel barked. "I have indulged you for the sake of our friendship. But you listen well...I am *Khalon*. My word is law. You would do well to remember that. I can always find another to replace you."

The pair stopped at the dead end of a hall and Bel tapped a device strapped to his forearm. Banji raised his stun rifle. If he eliminated Bel and Sta'ling, there was no telling how many lives he could save. Just as he was about to fire, a pop and a whoosh sounded as the wall behind the Tanis men wavered. Somehow a slip stream was opening up for them. The pair took a step back and disappeared.

"Damn it to the five hells!" Banji stepped out from their hiding place and paced around the area that Bel and Sta'ling had occupied just moments ago. He ran a frustrated hand though his hair. "*Frex!*"

"What just happened, Banji?" Maria hadn't yet been conscious when she traveled through a slip stream, so she didn't recognize it for what it was.

Banji lifted a hand at her, non-verbally telling her he didn't have time in that moment. He pulled a crystal communicator out of his pocket. This was one of the covert models that a user held to their throat. They could whisper and it would translate clearly across the device. In return, messages would vibrate in such a manner that it would echo in the receiver's head, but no one else could hear it. The only reason Maria know what it was was because Banji had shown all of the team how to use the newest model before they left the Tiaret military camp.

Of course she only heard one side of the conversation.

"Kavi, I need you to pass along some information to Reijo and Ghaleb. Tanis has functioning personal slip stream devices." He paused for a bit. "Yes, I'm sure.... Because I just saw the twice-damned thing being used.... How the *frex* should I know?... Does it really matter if we were told it was just in the concept stage?... Of course I know that this could be a game changer.... My priority it to get out of here alive, not grab you a new toy.... Fine. If I happen to come across one I will grab it, but honestly, you should have one of your spy network retrieve one."

Banji changed the frequency and shot off a second message to Allo. He told Allo and Boroff to start sending the women to safety. It meant that he and Maria would have to hurry if they had any hope of getting out of here with the rest of the team.

"We have to hurry," Banji stated. He stalked

over to where Maria was standing near the side hall that they had concealed themselves in. "I promise I will give you details when we have more time."

Maria nodded and Banji took her hand. She looked up, startled, when she felt a cold metal cylinder placed there.

"This is a laser blade. If you need a weapon press here." He used his finger to press hers into a switch. A hot beam of light shot out of the cylinder. "Move your thumb up and down and it will change the length from knife all the way to sword if necessary. The longer the beam the less cutting power it has, though even at maximum length it will cut through flesh."

Banji didn't know what they were going to face, and he knew that both he and Cleo would give their lives to protect Maria, but he felt better knowing she at least had a weapon at hand.

"You're going to have to lead the way, Maria. I'm moving blind here."

Maria raised a hand to Banji's cheek and pulled him down so she could place a kiss there. She knew putting her in harm's way went against every protective Banji had to rely on her.

"First floor, east wing…. That's where Sta'ling has his exam rooms. I noticed other labs through various doors when they were dragging me there. It stands to reason that the tissue storage would be near where they harvest it."

"Lead the way."

Maria pushed her aches and pains to the back of her mind once more and jogged down the corridor. She hung a right and then another left before she slowed down again. Maria started reading the signs tacked next to various doors.

She stepped into one that was labeled "processing." Inside Banji saw numerous lab stations.

"Tissue would need to be kept refrigerated or in some sort of stasis to keep it from decaying. Help me find something like that."

Banji searched until he found the control console. A few simple commands and a compartment in the back wall slid open. Banji wasn't a scientist, and he evidently forgot a step in opening the chamber because an alarm sounded and lights started flashing.

"Warning, stasis storage compromised. Stasis field failure in one minute."

The noise startled Cleo, who knocked over some nearby equipment. The sound of the equipment crashing sent the shesha into a panicked spin, where she continued to knock things over. Maria had to calm her down to extract her from the mess of broken equipment.

Banji pulled various canisters from the

storage unit. Each was neatly labeled with a number and then information about the sex, age, and health of the individual whose tissue it was.

"These all seem to be male samples."

Maria came over and confirmed what Banji was seeing. "These must be from the deformed phased he was experimenting on. These are all things like blood, muscle and skin. Stalin took my ovaries. I assume he did something similar to the other women."

"He took the entire organ?"

Banji was going to ask more questions, but a group of Tanis guards crashed into the lab. Banji should have known that the alarm would alert someone that they were here.

The first guard practically tripped over Cleo, who sunk her fangs into his leg before slithering out of the way. Banji concentrated on the men coming in after him. Thanks to Cleo's mess and the door to the lab, a bottleneck was created. The Tanis had no room to maneuver around their comrades, so Banji could deal with them almost one at a time. After repeated shots, his stunner ran out of power. He started using it like a club to give it time to recharge. He was able to take out nearly a half dozen Tanis soldiers before the final three surrounded him.

The Tanis had completely disregarded Maria as not being a threat. That was a mistake on their part. One of the soldiers surrounding Banji was within striking distance of Maria and had his back to her.

Maria pulled out the laser blade that Banji had given her and activated it. She took a deep breath before swinging the blade across the Achilles tendon at the back of the heel. The smell of burning leather and flesh filled the lab as the soldier screamed and collapsed to the ground.

That proved enough of a distraction to the other two that Banji was able to smash his elbow into one's face, knocking him out. He quickly grabbed the final soldier and wrenched his neck with a sickening crunch.

Banji grabbed the crippled man by his uniform and pulled him up until the whimpering man was nose to nose with him.

"Where is the artificial bio lab?"

The injured man glared at Banji in silence. Banji pressed the hilt of his own laser blade to the man's chest. If he activated it, the blade would impale the man, killing him. From the wide-eyed panic on the soldier's face, he knew it too.

"One more time…. Where is the artificial bio lab?"

The man whimpered. "Please don't kill me." Banji jabbed the hilt into the man's chest, causing him to flinch. "It's in…in the west wing. Sub level one."

Banji cold-cocked the man, knocking him out. He grabbed Maria's hand and pulled her into the hall. She was having trouble keeping up. Banji finally slowed down when his comm buzzed.

"What is it, Allo?"

"*Kijani*, the soldiers are starting to wake up. We have about half the women sent through. I estimate ten minutes more…at the most."

"We will do what we can, but you have your orders, Allo."

"Yes, sir."

"What's the artificial bio lab?" Maria asked before Banji could take off again.

"We don't really have time, Maria."

She crossed her arms and frowned. "Then you better make time."

"Fine. But I will have to tell you while we are on the move."

CHAPTER FORTY-ONE

"So the artificial bio lab mimics body processes to keep organs alive outside of the body?" Maria was having to hold her midsection as the pain there was getting worse from exertion.

"Basically. It was originally developed to keep patients alive, but the scientists discovered that it was possible to keep individual organs and tissues alive as well."

"Makes sense. Removing the ovaries would only yield a few viable eggs for fertilization. But if you could keep the process going, allowing them to mature, you have a potentially thousands of future offspring."

They stopped at the stairwell that would lead them to sub level one. They hadn't encountered anyone on their way here. It should have been a blessing considering their time crunch, but Banji had a bad feeling. They should have had to at least avoid soldiers. Banji knew that they were waking up and he had also seen Sta'ling order soldiers to secure the inventory. If the genetic material from the women was the inventory he was referring to, then they should have run across someone by now.

Banji took point going down the stairs, with Maria in the middle and Cleo bringing up the rear. The shesha had proven to be invaluable because of its loyalty. If they made it back...no, when, not if, they made it back, Banji would discuss with Reijo the possibility of having trained teams of envenomed shesha and handlers within the military ranks.

Even at the base of the stairs, the way was disconcertingly clear. If Banji hadn't understood how important this was to Maria, he would have turned them around and double timed it to the slip stream.

"Seven minutes," Banji whispered. That was their time limit. It meant they had a few minutes at best to get what they needed and get out of there.

Banji entered the artificial bio lab. Along the walls were compartments meant to house various body parts with clear crystal fronts to observe inside. The room itself was cast into a blue tinged glow, as the only light came from within those compartments. Maria walked around the room while Banji turned. With each empty compartment, the tickle of unease at the back of Banji's mind increased. The fact that hundreds of compartments were empty, save one, did not bode well for them. Cleo's rattle sounded softly. Evidently he wasn't the only one feeling nervous.

Banji's guard went up as Maria went to the compartment glowing red, meaning it wasn't empty. She pressed the crystal display. It took her a little longer to read the information since her translator had to convert the language to one she would recognize.

"Subject: human. Sex: female. Age: approximately twenty-eight solars…I suppose that is similar to an Earth year?"

"Yes it is," Banji responded. He kept eyeing the shadows in the room. He felt like they were being watched.

"Then this is probably me. Does your planet have the technology to restore this and give me the chance to have children one day?"

"If the organs are still healthy and yours, then yes." Banji watched Maria. He had never really thought about fathering children, but watching the wistfulness in Maria's eyes made him want to have a child if it was with her.

Maria reached out and laid her hand on the window of the compartment, "Though I suppose a DNA test would have to confirm it."

"No need for that, M'lady. I can confirm that

those reproductive organs are indeed yours." Sta'ling Tanis' shadow filled the doorway, flanked by the two guards they saw him with earlier. "I knew you would be back. You are resourceful but predictable."

Banji started to raise the stunner he held in his hands.

"I don't think so." Sta'ling raised an unfamiliar weapon and aimed it right at Maria. "Our newest prototype. It tears apart the body on the atomic level from the inside out. From what I have observed, it seems excruciatingly painful, and a hit anywhere is fatal." He waved the weapon at Maria. "Put down all of your weapons or you can watch your mate die in agony."

Banji threw the stunner away from him and dropped the laser blade. Sta'ling gestured to continue, so Banji removed a few hidden knives and gently placed Daya's explosive device on a nearby table.

"The hidden garrote as well." Banji lifted a brow in surprise and Sta'ling smirked. "Didn't think I would know about that little toy did you? Well your brother basically decapitated one of my men with it, and I would rather not have a repeat." The soldiers behind Sta'ling rubbed their neck and eyed Banji as he pulled the thin wire from the seam it was sewn into.

Sta'ling kept his eyes on Banji but called out

to his men, "Take the Tiaret spy into custody. Bel wants him alive. He's an exact copy of his brother, so he should be just as profi…. Agh!"

The enemy had forgotten the silent shesha. Cleo had slithered around the room and struck Sta'lin's forearm. The weapon dropped to the floor with a clatter, and Cleo's tail flicked it away. Sta'ling grabbed his injured arm and yelled at his soldiers to get them.

The men were armed with stun sticks because Sta'ling didn't want the pulse rifle to damage the sensitive scientific equipment. Unfortunately for the soldiers, that meant that they would have to get up close and personal with Banji. Banji just grinned. Hand to hand combat was his specialty.

The men were smart enough to come at him both at the same time. They had hoped to distract or overwhelm Banji. Banji blocked the stun stick of the man to his left. He slid his hand up its shaft and then twisted it out of the soldier's grasp. He used the back handle to give that soldier a blow to the head that staggered him. He then twisted and spun the weapon to face the second man. They jousted with the stun sticks, neither one getting close enough to shock the other. This one was the better trained fighter of the pair.

The weaponless soldier tried to punch Banji in the side, but Banji had kept him in his peripheral because he knew that he hadn't knocked him out and side-stepped him. The move had the soldier off balance, and Banji kicked him in the back of the knee, sending him to the ground. He quickly stunned him in the back of the neck, rendering the man unconscious. Cleo quietly finished him off.

The second soldier took advantage of Banji's distraction and hit him with the stun stick in the side. The shock jolted Banji's body but to the soldier's horror did not bring him down. Once again, being tortured by Kavi's training regime proved useful.

Banji's opponent was smart. When he figured out that stunning Banji wasn't going to work, he knocked Banji's weapon from his hands. He then tackled Banji and used the stun stick to press down on Banji's throat. The move restricted some of Banji's air, but he was saved from being completely strangled by his battle collar.

Banji reached up and gouged at his attacker's eyes. The Tanis soldier howled in pain and grabbed his face, allowing Banji to buck him off. Banji switched positions, pinning the man beneath him. The fight quickly turned into a grabbling match. Each man would have the advantage for a moment before the other would reverse position. It was an impressive display of wrestling prowess.

Banji finally pinned the other man beneath him, using his legs to keep his opponent's arms immobile. The man continued to try and buck Banji off; it was like trying to ride a rabid ghost lion. Banji grabbed the man on either side of his head and snapped his neck. With one last jerk, the man beneath him stilled. Banji looked down and panted from exertion. He was getting too old for this kind of thing.

"No!"

Banji turned at Maria's scream. He watched in horror as a shaky Sta'ling charged at him, brandishing a metallic blade. Maria ran to his defense. Banji turned to face the attack. Everything seemed to be happening in slow motion, but Banji knew that it was a matter of seconds. The blade arched down towards Banji as he brought his arm up to deflect it. Suddenly Maria was in between him and Sta'ling, wrapping her arms protectively around Banji.

She cried out as the blade sank into her back. Banji held her in shock. She had protected him. He was supposed to be the one who protected her. His hands were warm with her blood. He tried to staunch the flow in vain.

Sta'ling staggered towards the exit. "Well I suppose we won't be needing this anymore." He punched in a code on the compartment containing Maria's ovaries. "They do us no good if the woman is dead; we need a genetically compatible incubator after all."

"Purging fifteen alpha," a computerized voice announced as a bright flash of light filled the artificial bio lab. When the light faded, the compartment containing Maria's genetic material glowed blue like the rest of the empty containers.

Maria lifted a bloody hand to Banji's face and gave him a wan smile. "No regrets. I love you."

Tears flowed down Banji's cheek. "No, you can't leave me…not yet. I need you."

Maria caressed his cheek before her eyes fluttered closed and her hand went limp. Her breathing was shallow, but she was still alive.

"Such a touching scene. I wonder if this will ultimately break you or make you the predator you are meant to be." Sta'ling gave a shaky laugh as he moved to leave. "I'll be watching the results with anticipation."

Banji gently laid the dying Maria on the ground. He stood, scooping up the laser blade as he went. He stalked toward Sta'ling. Sta'ling realized he was facing down his death and quickly started programming the device on his wrist. Unfortunately for him, Cleo's poison may not have killed him but it made his movements clumsy.

He pushed the last command and watched in fascinated horror as the bright blade sliced through his own neck. A pop and a whoosh and Sta'ling disappeared, minus his head, which rolled across the lab floor with shocked eyes.

CHAPTER FORTY-TWO

Banji dropped next to Maria. Her breathing was becoming labored and she was deathly pale from blood loss. If he could get her to the regeneration units, she might live. But moving her would surely kill her.

Then Banji remembered what Elod and Hikamet had kept in the palace's medical facility. When they had to transport a severely injured person, they often put a stasis unit on them. It kept the body from degrading further by putting all of the organs and functions into a frozen state. It wouldn't keep that person alive forever if they were mortally wounded, but it would buy a few hours.

There had to be a stasis unit somewhere in here; his only worry was finding one large enough to cover an entire person instead of just a single organ. It was the artificial bio lab after all. Banji checked Maria one last time before he started tearing through the disaster of a lab.

Thank the gods for overly organized scientists. Banji stumbled upon an inventory list with locations. The drawer that contained the large stasis generator was located near the exit. He found it but it was jammed shut thanks to the battle that took place here. Banji kicked the twice damned thing in frustration. He turned to find something to pry it open with when he heard the lock disengage and the drawer hiss open.

He grabbed the generator and checked how much energy it had. It wasn't fully charged; he would have maybe half an hour before the field started to fail. It didn't give Maria much of a chance, but it was at least a chance.

He slapped the generator over Maria's wound and turned it on. Immediately the blood stopped flowing and Maria stopped breathing as the shimmer of nanoparticles raced across her body.

While the device worked its magic, Banji armed Daya's little toy. Banji wasn't going to let the Tanis use this facility against the population again. He tossed the bomb into the far corner and started counting down in his head. It would take a few more seconds for the stasis field to encase Maria. When the stasis field covered her entire body, Banji carefully lifted Maria in his arms.

He took off at a run; they had only a few

minutes left before Allo and the others would leave without them and they had to get out of the building as soon as possible. If they didn't make it, then Maria died and nothing else mattered.

"Come on, Cleo," Banji called the large serpent. With his hands full, he was going to have to count on the shesha to defend them if necessary. Cleo took off, pulling ahead of Banji. She hissed and snapped with her tail rattling loudly. It was almost comical to see the bleary-eyed Tanis jump out of her way.

They made it through the medical facility and out the doors just as the ground shook with a massive explosion. Banji didn't turn back to see how much of the building remained. He honestly didn't care. The streets of the outpost were starting to swarm with the Tanis personnel that finally woke up from their induced sleep.

Without Sta'ling or Bel, there was no clear leadership and the foot soldiers were running around in the confusion without direction. Cleo snapped at a nearby soldier, who tripped over his comrade trying to get away. For the most part, the Tanis seemed more concerned with battling the fires caused by the explosions and trying to organize themselves. The few that tried to challenge Banji were easily dissuaded by Cleo.

Banji's communicator vibrated in his pocket.

He didn't answer it but was fairly certain it was the team trying to contact him to let him know that all of the women were through. If that was the case, they had moments to get to the slip stream before Banji would be trapped here with a dying Maria.

Banji shifted Maria in his arms and put on a burst of speed. The building that housed the slip stream depot was just ahead. It looked like he was going to make it free and clear—until a phased soldier stood right in front of the doors.

By the two moons, Banji didn't have time for this. Instead of stopping to fight, he ran up some nearby debris and then launched himself over the man standing in his way. He ran full tilt and turned just enough to protect Maria's body and slam his shoulder into the doors, flinging them open.

The slip stream was activated and Banji saw Boroff disappear. They had just barely made it. A flashing light on the control console alerted Banji to the fact that Daya's solution for not leaving a man behind was counting down.

Cleo slithered by Banji and was quickly sucked into the event horizon of the slip stream, disappearing right after Boroff. Banji didn't even try to fight the pull of the slip stream sucking him in. The last thing he saw was the phased and a few others bursting into the building before he experienced the disorienting shifting of the slip stream.

*****

It only takes a few moments to send someone to the other side of the planet. But in those few moments, Banji felt the percussive force of the console exploding, preventing their enemy from following them.

That force blow Banji and Maria across the slip stream room in Kavi's secret training facility. Banji wrapped his body around Maria's, trying to protect her from the impact. He hit the far wall as the slip stream collapsed and warnings blared.

Allo and Boroff ran to him, overjoyed that they had made it. Their smiling faces fell when they saw the state Maria was in. Kavi shoved through the crowd of confused females and stalked towards Banji. The old man could be an intimidating presence when he wanted to be.

Banji stood and cut Kavi off before he could start. "You can have me arrested later." He held out Maria in front of him. "Her stasis field is failing from the blast. She needs to get to medical now."

Kavi whistled loudly and a pair of medics that had been assessing the women ran over to Banji. Someone called a medical emergency and more medics were on their way with a transport cart.

"She's got something clutched in her hand," Banji heard one of the medics say. He leaned over

318

and almost laughed. Even when dying Maria was thinking ahead. Banji pried the prototype weapon from Maria's fingers and let the medics load her up and take her away.

Kavi started to yell at him and Banji shoved the tool into his mentor's hands.

"What in the five hells is this?" Kavi demanded.

"Prototype of a new Tanis weapon. Better get the engineers on finding a way to counter or protect from it because if it does what Sta'ling said it does, it will allow the Tanis to decimate our forces without breaking a sweat."

"I don't suppose you got the personal slip stream like I asked for?"

Banji glared at Kavi and started to follow the path the medics took.

"Where do you think you are going?"

Banji didn't even look back. "I'm going to be by the side of my mate."

"You aren't going anywhere until I say you can. Damn it, this is important, Banji," Kavi yelled after him.

Banji just lifted his arm in a farewell wave. "That is where you are wrong, Kavi. The only thing that is important was hauled out of here to medical. Everything else doesn't matter." He walked out to stand vigil in medical until he knew Maria would be all right.

It was there that Allo found him a few hours later. Cleo curled up at his feet.

"Do they allow pets in here?" Allo made himself known at the door.

Banji looked up and smiled sadly as he stroked Cleo's head. "They tried to remove her, but when she hissed at the orderly they decided to leave her alone."

"Any word yet?" Allo sat beside his friend and commander.

"They were almost finished with the surgery and regeneration. The blade destroyed one kidney and nicked an artery. Her body was beginning to shut down due to blood loss before I got the stasis generator on her." Banji leaned his head against the wall, banging it a couple of times in frustration. "The next day or two will be critical. If she remains stable she should be okay, but the head medic warned that it was possible that her body could just shut down from all of the trauma she has suffered."

"If she is still alive now, then she will be fine." Banji gave his friend a side-eyed look. "Think about it. The Tanis were never able to break her. She threw herself into harm's way to protect someone she loves. Maria is a fighter…no not like Megan or you, but she has a strength all her own."

Banji nodded and then changed the subject.

"I didn't see Daya when we came through. Did he make it back?" Banji felt kind of guilty that he hadn't checked up on his men yet.

Allo rubbed the back of his neck, "Umm...not exactly."

Banji just raised a brow in question.

"Evidently Maria's friend felt she owed Bel a 'blood debt' and refused to come here until it was repaid. Daya decided to keep her out of trouble and followed her when she took off."

"I'm sure I will hear about him taking off on his own from Kavi and Reijo."

"As far as they know he was acting on your orders."

"You lied to your superiors for me?"

"Lie is such a strong word. I prefer embellishing the truth based on knowledge garnered from a longstanding friendship."

"*Kijani* Banji." The orderly sent to retrieve him recoiled in fear when Cleo uncoiled and raised her head.

"Has there been a change?" The worry in Banji's voice focused the scared young man.

"N...no, sir. Chief Medic Sorel sent me to let you know that she has been settled comfortably in a room, if you want to go back with her now."

Banji and Allo stood and clasped hands.

"I'll keep the buzzard raptors at bay a little

longer. Go take care of your mate."

"Thank you, Allo."

CHAPTER FORTY-THREE

She floated through the darkness. In the distance she could hear voices and see a faint light. A few times she tried to get closer to those voices because it seemed terribly important for some reason, but the closer she got the more it hurt. So she retreated to the darkness where she felt no pain.

"You have to fight through the pain, *nipotina.*"

"Nonno, you shouldn't be here." A hazy image of her grandfather started to form. "I left you behind on Earth."

"I'm not on Earth any longer, child. My time has passed."

Maria felt tears run down her cheeks.

"I'm so sorry. I left you," she sobbed. "It's all my fault."

"Nonsense, *piccolo*. I was an old man. My time would have been done whether you were there or not." Maria's grandfather solidified in the darkness and she felt him wrap his arms around her in a strong hug. "No, you are right where god meant you to be."

The voices became louder and a wave of pain wracked Maria's body.

"It hurts, *Nonno*."

"I know it does; but the pain will eventually fade. You just have to decide if the pain is worth what awaits you."

"Maria, *jinaria*…you can't leave me." A voice echoed from the light.

Maria knew that voice, but she couldn't remember why. It seemed very important that she remember. Every time the memory came close, pain would fill her mind and she would retreat again.

"If you go, my love, I will follow." He shouldn't follow her; she was dying and Maria needed him to be safe—though she wasn't sure why.

"Remember my child."

Maria's grandfather touched her temple and in a blinding flash she remembered…everything. All the pain, all of the suffering, but she also remembered the joy and the love.

"Banji…" she whispered.

"Yes, Banji, *piccolo*. You sacrificed yourself

for him." Maria's grandfather stroked her face and she leaned into his comforting touch. "Tell me was he worth dying for?"

Without hesitation Maria answered, "Yes!"

"Then he is worth living for."

With that statement, Maria's grandfather shoved her into the pain and light she had been avoiding. She cried out and reached for her grandfather because she knew in her heart that this would be the last time she saw him. He simply smiled at her and waved goodbye.

CHAPTER FORTY-FOUR

Banji was sitting beside Maria's bedside like he had every day for the last week. For the first couple of days, Maria had been hooked up to machines that took over the functions of her ruined organs, while technicians grew new ones from her own genetic material. They had surgically implanted the new organs a few days ago and the chief medic claimed the operation was a success. So far they seemed to be functioning fine.

Sorel, the chief medic, was growing more concerned by the day. He couldn't find an explanation for Maria's comatose state. There was no swelling of the brain. They had restored her blood levels and her injuries and surgery were healing nicely. There was no medical reason for Maria to still be unconscious.

The chief medic could only guess at this point, but he surmised that Maria hadn't woken up because she needed a psychological break from the trauma she had endured these many months. Brain scans showed that her mind was actively working, as if she was in a dream state. He was still hopeful that she would wake on her own after her mind had processed everything. Banji had a feeling that the longer Maria remained unconscious, the harder it would be for her to wake up.

So he talked to her. He told her about his life growing up in the warrior's den. He talked about his brother and how much he missed him and his fear that he would never see him again. He told her how much she meant to him and how life wouldn't be worth living without her. He talked to her until his voice was hoarse from use. Yet she just lay there so still.

Allo and Boroff visited fairly regularly. If it wasn't for Allo, Banji probably wouldn't eat on a regular basis. Even Kavi and Reijo came to check on him. Reijo seemed to be the only one who understood his vigilance.

Banji was reduced to pleading with Maria. He laid his head upon her stomach and wept. Banji never cried. He was the joker, the false bravado…he faced his fears by making light of them. But he couldn't do that with Maria. Somehow this woman had wormed her way inside and now held a part of Banji's soul. If he were to lose her, he would lose a part of himself.

Then he felt her body twitch. The medic said that was when her consciousness was closer to the surface. Banji looked up at her face and saw tears leaking from her eyes.

"Maria, *jinaria*…you can't leave me." Banji begged, and her fingers squeezed the hand that had been holding them for days.

Banji started begging in earnest. He stroked her face and kissed her lips as she went slack again; he was losing her.

"If you go, my love, I will follow," Banji threatened.

Her hand squeezed his once more and the monitors started wailing because her heart rate increased so dramatically.

"Banji…" the whispered name uttered from her lips was mana from heaven as far as he was concerned.

"I'm here, Maria. Come back to me my love. I need you ever so much." Banji sobbed as he watched her eyes, hoping for some indication that she was finally awake. Sorel and his assistant bust into the room to check on what was causing the frighteningly fast heart rate.

Maria sat bolt upright in the bed as she awoke with a pained scream. Her sudden movement knocked Sorel's handheld scanner from his grasp and across the room. Maria grabbed her midsection and her scream reduced to clenched teeth panting.

"Analgesic, now!" Sorel called to his assistant, who promptly placed a pressure syringe into his hand. Sorel quickly administered the pain-relieving drug, and within moments Maria relaxed and allowed Sorel and Banji to lie her back down on the bed.

Sorel retrieved his scanner and checked the diagnostics to make sure it wasn't damaged. When he was certain it was fine, he turned to Maria.

"Let's see if all of my delicate work is intact. Newly grown kidneys can be a bit sensitive."

Sorel scanned Maria and smiled, seemingly satisfied with what he was reading.

"Were you able to restore my ovaries?" Maria's voice croaked from disuse.

Sorel shook his head and frowned, "I'm sorry, that is one organ that we cannot successfully create in a lab."

"But Banji said you should be able to put back in what Sta'ling took out."

Banji lifted Maria's hand to his lips. When she looked at him she saw sadness and regret.

"*Jinaria*, I'm afraid that Sta'ling destroyed your ovaries as you lay dying. I'm so sorry. I wasn't able to stop him."

Maria pulled her hand from Banji's grasp.

The Vukasin people needed women who could bear children to keep the population going. It wasn't fair to expect Banji to remain with her if she couldn't have children.

Banji grabbed Maria's face with both hands and forced her to look at him. He laid his forehead against hers.

"You are thinking too much, my love."

"You need children, *amore mio*." She reached up a hand to cup his cheek.

Tears streaked down both Banji's and Maria's faces. Banji kissed the side of Maria's mouth.

"I need you. If all I have is you, that is more than enough."

Sorel coughed, "Well…um…."

Maria turned to look at the man who had saved her life.

"Here's the thing…you're pregnant. I'd estimate about six weeks along."

"How?" Banji asked.

Maria pinched the bridge of her nose and laughed, "The hormone injections from the prison." The color leeched from Maria's face as she realized that the child may not be Banji's. "Can we test who the father is?"

Banji wrapped his arms around Maria's shoulder and hugged her tight. "*Jinaria*, it doesn't matter. The child is a part of you and I will love it no matter what."

Sorel smiled. "Well, we can of course test paternity if it would make you feel better, but I am fairly certain that Banji is the father."

"How can you be so sure?" Maria asked.

"Because you are carrying twins!"

EPILOGUE

Maria sat in the garden of the royal palace a few months later. She was now heavily pregnant, and Sorel insisted on being on hand to closely monitor her. Maria stroked her growing tummy and thought about how much life had changed.

Kavi hadn't been happy when Banji refused to go back into the field. After all they had been through, he didn't want to be away from Maria for any length of time. But Maria knew that if they received reliable news of his brother, Akia, that Banji would most likely go. She couldn't fault him for that. Family, after all, was everything.

Maria told Banji about the vision of her grandfather, and he held her as she grieved. Maria firmly believed that the vision was real and her grandfather had died. In a way it was something she needed to know so she could live her life here on Vukas without regrets. She was finally at the point that she could remember the good things without breaking down into tears. It had helped that Banji had suggested calling one of the twins Alberto after her grandfather.

Many of the women from Ludus Prime had been able to give Ghaleb and Reijo information about what the Tanis had been doing and for how long. The Tanis had been grooming the other planet for years and now basically controlled everything there. They were actively seeking contact and relations with other species. This could easily tip the scales against the Ivalio and Vukas in the looming conflict. Because of this information, the council voted to increase the scope of the war effort to include liberating Ludus Prime. When it was safe, the women would have the choice whether to return to their planet or remain on Vukas.

Kavi had finally convinced Banji to act as an instructor for new field operatives. That was how they had found themselves living at the royal palace.

"Are you ready?" Megan emerged from the palace wearing a beautiful dress of sapphire blue. She held two bouquets in her hands. "You still have time to run for the hills," she teased.

Maria stood; it wouldn't be long before she would need help for such a simple task. She brushed the wrinkles from her flowing white gown.

Megan handed her one of the bouquets. "I can't believe you convinced Banji to have a wedding ceremony. As far as the Vukasins are concerned the mating bite is more than enough."

Maria smiled. Banji was working overtime to make sure that she was happy. When she had explained about weddings and how she had dreamed of hers as a little girl, he had insisted that she have one. He had even bullied Reijo and Ghaleb into helping to make it happen.

"He wants to make me happy," Maria said wistfully.

"Well we had better go before he sends the troops to look for you. I have never seen a more nervous groom." Megan laughed.

Maria looked up at the twilight sky. Both moons already shown brightly. Yes, N*onno* was right. She was right where she was meant to be.

"Let's go." Maria walked through the palace doors and into her future.

ABOUT THE AUTHOR

B.D. Snowden is a Texas native living in the Great Plains with her children of both two-legged and four-legged varieties. She is a voracious reader whose book habit literally brought a small town library to life. One day, when she was unable to get something new to read, she started turning the stories floating through her head into concrete concepts on paper. Find information about new releases and appearances at:
Geekygothblog.wordpress.com
Facebook.com/BrandiceSnowdenWriter

www.ingramcontent.com/pod-product-compliance
Lightning Source LLC
Chambersburg PA
CBHW061325170626
46817CB00001B/311